William A. Cook

## Opinions and Practice of the Founders of the Republic

The administration of Abraham Lincoln sustained by the sages and heroes

of the revolution

William A. Cook

**Opinions and Practice of the Founders of the Republic**
*The administration of Abraham Lincoln sustained by the sages and heroes of the revolution*

ISBN/EAN: 9783337195090

Printed in Europe, USA, Canada, Australia, Japan

Cover: Foto ©Andreas Hilbeck / pixelio.de

More available books at **www.hansebooks.com**

# OPINIONS AND PRACTICE

OF THE

# Founders of the Republic,

IN RELATION TO

## Arbitrary Arrests, Imprisonment of Tories, Writ of Habeas Corpus, Seizure of Arms and of Private Papers, Domiciliary Visits, Confiscation of Real and Personal Estate, etc., etc.

OR,

# THE ADMINISTRATION OF ABRAHAM LINCOLN

SUSTAINED

## BY THE SAGES AND HEROES OF THE REVOLUTION.

———

" In settling that which is uncertain, in law and politics, and, therefore in construction likewise, great aid is derived from precedents and authorities."   LIEBER.

"I am sure, the mass of citizens in these United States mean well; and I firmly believe they will always *act well*, whenever they *can obtain a right understanding of matters.*"
WASHINGTON.

"There is a responsibility for ignorant censorship as well as for learned perversion. He who would instruct, must be careful to be instructed.  He who is instructed, must be careful to make his statements fair and full."   COLWELL.

———

BY WILLIAM A. COOK.

WASHINGTON, D. C.
WILLIAM H. MOORE, PRINTER, 484 ELEVENTH STREET.
1864.

# Address to the Reader.

STAY, READER. You are a citizen of the United States. Your country is passing through a fearful crisis. It may be in danger of perishing. It may disappear from the map of nations. Its flag may cease to float among the banners of the world.

Would you assist in preventing these melancholy results? Who can doubt it? Turn not away then from this tract. Dash it not down unread.

It contains important truths. It is the product of hours of patient toil. In its preparation numerous volumes and thousands of pages have been examined. It is not a mass of wild declamation. It does not consist of individual opinions and theories. It leads you in "a plain and easy way" among the fathers of the Republic. It places you in their council chambers. It gives you their views and practice relative to arbitrary arrests, imprisonments, the writ of *habeas corpus*, confiscation of property, and other equally important matters.

It shows you what they considered should be done in the hour of national conflict and struggle!

Is not this exactly what you wish to learn and understand? Surely it is. As Washington, Franklin, Jefferson, Henry, Adams, and their associates were patriots, you desire to be a patriot. As they were honest, you would be honest. If you have erroneous prejudices you would lay them on the altar of your country. For no man, no faction, no party, no reward, would you sacrifice it. Let no one then mislead you.

Read, examine these pages with a candid mind. If you find that they contain facts, surrender your mind to their control. If, upon a careful perusal, you find them filled with falsehood and error, reject them.

Act nobly. Determine to do right no matter what it may cost; no matter what associations may be abandoned or what ties may be severed. By such a determination and corresponding action duty will be performed, and living and dying hours be blessed. For after all, "THE GRANDEST AND HOLIEST THING IN THE UNIVERSE IS TO DO RIGHT."

---

☞ Facilities for the preparation of this tract have been furnished by Hon. J. M. EDMUNDS, Commissioner of the General Land Office, and by Hon. W. T. OTTO, Assistant Secretary of the Interior.

Both have been persistent and energetic in their efforts to sustain the Government in her extraordinary contest with armed and unarmed foes. In copying a mass of matter, *amply sufficient for a ponderous volume*, and to some extent in the selection of that part of it which is included in the tract, Geo. W. Smith of Pennsylvania, John R. Brown of Virginia, Chas. M. Heaton, Frank M. Heaton, and T. F. Stokes of Indiana, and Henry Taylor, of Washington, D. C., have rendered efficient aid.

It may be added that among the works which have been particularly consulted or quoted are the following, viz: Journals of Continental Congress, IV volumes; American Archives, fourth and fifth series; Elliott's Debates, Documentary History of New York, Pennsylvania Archives and Colonial Records, Henneng's Virginia Statutes at Large, the writings of Washington, Irving's Life of Washington, Life and Works of John Adams, Jefferson's Works, Hamilton's Works, Franklin's Works, Life of Governor Morris, Life of Jay, Life and times of James Madison, by Reves; Loyalists of America, and Revolutionary pamphlets.

# PART I.

THE NATURE OF THE REVOLUTIONARY STRUGGLE.—THE NUMBER OF THE DISAFFECTED.—THE INQUIRY PROPOUNDED AS TO THE MODE IN WHICH THEY WERE TREATED BY THE FOUNDERS OF THE REPUBLIC, ETC.

Good and evil—right and wrong—truth and falsehood—liberty and slavery—have contended for ages.

The struggle of the American colonies for independence was simply a battle between these opposing forces.

It is a remarkable fact, sustained by both sacred and profane history, that in all such contests true principles and correct purposes have encountered unexpected and unnatural opposition.

From their own ranks have arisen inveterate and unprincipled foes. It was so in the Revolutionary age. *Then, as now,* there were traitors in the land. *Then, as now,* political malcontents and grumblers—traducers of "those in authority"—and of the armed warriors of freedom, plotted in secret, and at times spoke out in social gatherings and public assemblies. *And as George the III and the British government then had their supporters, sympathizers, and eulogists, so has Jeff. Davis and the Southern Confederacy to-day.*

Nor were these "internal enemies" few in number. They were numerous, far more so than is commonly supposed.

Sabine, in his "Loyalists of the American Revolution," states that "the friends of independence were a minority in some of the States, barely equalled their opponents in others, and in the whole country composed but an inconsiderable majority; and that a very considerable proportion of the professional and editorial intelligence and talents of the thirteen colonies was arrayed against the popular movement."

And he concludes from the best evidence he could obtain that there were "twenty-five thousand," at the lowest computation, "who took up arms on the side of the Crown,"

And John Adams, Life and Works, vol. x, page 193, asserts, that "*a party in favor of Great Britain was formed and organized and drilled and disciplined* to the extent of nearly one-third of the people of the colonies.

*The questions then arises, what were the opinions of the founders of the Republic relative to "this party"* —THE TORIES OF THEIR DAY—*and in what manner did they deal with them or act toward them?* Correct information on these points is of primary importance. It will tend to silence the clamors of the Peace-War democracy relative to *arbitrary arrests, imprisonment of conspirators and traitors, or of those suspected of these crimes, the suspension of the writ of habeas corpus, disarming of persons hostile to the purposes and operations of the Government, seizure of correspondence or papers, domiciliary visits or searching of houses, restraint upon travel, the use of private property, confiscation of real and personal estate, the control of elections, the use and maintenance of governmental currency, interference with religion, retaliation for cruelties toward prisoners of war, exclusion of disloyal employees from office, and test oaths.*

It will convict their orators and conventions of profound ignorance, or wilful perversion of the views of "the Fathers"—on all of these and kindred topics. It will justify the leading measures of the Administration, and clearly evince that Mr. Lincoln, his Cabinet, and the majority of the Congress, have "comprehended and been inspired by the true spirit and genius of the Government." It will show that they are indeed the regular successors in the ranks of liberty, of Washington, and his compeers, both civil and military.

In presenting this information much

of value will be omitted. Condensation will be aimed at. First the views and acts of "the Continental Congress" will be given. Then those of several of the "colonies" will be presented. These will be found to harmonize—the one in fact growing out of the other. To these may be added, in conclusion, the views of the most distinguished of the founders of our nationality. As far as possible the subjects will be classified, and indicated by appropriate titles, or "head lines." In order to allay suspicion as to their authenticity and genuineness, each quotation will be sustained by reference to the volume from which it shall be taken.

## CONTINENTAL CONGRESS.

This representative assembly met originally in Carpenter's Hall, Philadelphia, on the 5th of September, 1774.

"It was the first in a succession of congresses," the sessions of which were held in each year during the period of the Revolutionary war.

From this body emanated "The Declaration of Independence," "The Articles of Confederation," and other papers of rare and permanent political value. Its deliberations were adorned and strengthened by talents, knowledge and virtues of the highest order.

Rash and profane, therefore, would he be who would assert or intimate that the "American Congress" was ignorant of the true principles of human liberty, or indifferent as respects "the rights of man."

It was to define, vindicate, and secure these that it assembled, and in the earnestness and sincerity of their purposes its members in the second year of its existence formally "pledged to each other their lives, their fortunes, and their sacred honor."

Inspired and controlled by these great objects, looking to their ultimate attainment, it was deemed of the very first importance "to discover, detect, and expose all who manifested hostility to them." Hence, in the outset of its deliberations, in the "plan of association" adopted and signed on Thursday, October 20th, 1774," this provision is found:

"ARTICLE 11. That a committee be chosen in every county, city, and town, by those who are qualified to vote for representatives in the legislature, *whose business it shall be attentively to observe the conduct of all persons touching this association,* and when it shall be made to appear to the satisfaction of a majority of any such committee, that any person within the limits of their appointment has violated this association that this majority *do forthwith cause the truth of the case to be published in the Gazette, to the end that all such foes to the rights of British America may be publicly known and universally contemned as the enemies of American liberty;* and thenceforth we respectively will break off all dealings with him or her.—Jour. Con., page 25, volume I. Thursday, October 20, 1774."

But this provision was found to be defective; measures more *positive*, *stringent*, and *radical*, were required, and they were shortly adopted, and energetically pursued. Let them be particularly exhibited.

## CHAPTER I.

### ARBITRARY ARRESTS.

On no topic do "the enemies of the Government" declaim more frequently and vociferously than on this. The phrase "arbitrary arrests" leaps from their lips with alarming velocity, and excited intonations, and stands forth in their pamphlets and newspapers in leaded lines and extended capitals. What does it mean? *Simply an arrest of individuals suspected of offenses without the ordinary formalities of a previous oath and warrant. Or in other terms, a prompt and discretionary seizure of persons known, or supposed, to be guilty of crimes.* Now, notwithstanding the inflamatory vociferations and solemn appeals of "modern democracy," the sages of the Revolution authorized and justified such arrests. Here is the proof:

"*Resolved*, That it be recommended to the several provincial assemblies, or conventions, and councils, or committees of safety, TO ARREST AND SECURE every person in their respective colonies whose going at large may, IN THEIR OPINION, endanger the safety of the Colony, or the liberties of America.—Jour. Con., vol. 1, p. 149."

What could be more conclusive? This "recommended" the *arrest* of all whose "going at large," in *the opinion* of the regularly constituted loyal assembly, might endanger the contest for freedom. That *opinion*, of itself, was regarded as a sufficient basis of arrest. And so it continued to be considered until the Treaty of Peace of 1783.

It appeared, however, that in some instances arrests were rashly made

* Arrests, *without warrants*, may be made either by officers or private persons, especially in cases of TREASON or *felony*. This may be done to "*prevent* crime as well as to detain a criminal." To justify it, "*reasonable and probable ground of suspicion* is sufficient." The common idea that in all cases warrants must precede arrests is unfounded. Every day they are made without any special authority, by municipal and other civil officers.—Sharswood's Blackstone Commentaries, vol. 2, book 4, chap. XXI, *Arrests, and notes*; Bouvier's Law Doc., article *Arrest*.

In referring to "Government arrests," these fundamental legal principles are artfully concealed or mis-stated by partizans.

by individuals. To prevent this, on June, 1776, the following regulation was adopted:

"*Resolved*, That no man in these Colonies charged with being a Tory, or unfriendly to the cause of American liberty, be injured in his person or property, or in any manner whatever disturbed, unless the proceeding against him be founded on an order of this Congress, or the Assembly, Convention, Council, or Committee of Safety of the Colony, or Committee of Inspection and Observation of the district where he resides; provided that *this resolution shall not prevent the apprehending of any person found in the commission of some act destructive of American liberty, or justly suspected of a design to commit such act*," &c.

Two things should here be observed. First, that in "*extreme cases*" arrests by individuals were allowed; and, second, that the Continental Congress retained or assumed concurrent jurisdiction with the several Colonies over "Tories, or persons unfriendly to the cause of America."

The doctrine of "*exclusive local control over all internal or domestic affairs*" belongs to a later, and a degenerate, period.

Congress continuing energetic and vigilant in 1777 this action was had, viz:

"*Resolved*, That it be recommended to the executive powers of the respective States, *forthwith to apprehend* and secure all persons * * * * * who have, *in their general conduct and conversation, evinced a disposition inimical to the cause of America;* and that the persons so seized be confined in such places, and treated in such manner, as shall be consistent with their respective characters, and security of their persons.—Jour, Cong., vol. II, p. 246.

Let it be distinctly noted, that this contemplated an *immediate* apprehension. No hesitancy, no delay, was sanctioned. And the existence of "*a disposition* inimical to the American cause" manifested by "*general conduct and conversation*," was deemed sufficient to justify a "seizure of person." "*Overt acts,*" *specific doings*, were not deemed indispensable. Moreover the recommended "seizure" was to be by "the Executive power."

These particulars cannot be too closely studied. Others, however, of no less importance will appear. In a most critical period of the contest for independence "this" preamble and resolution were passed:

. "Whereas, the States of Pennsylvania and Delaware are *threatened* with an immediate invasion from a powerful army, who have already landed at the head of Chesapeake bay; *and whereas the principles of policy and self-preservation require that all persons who may be reasonably suspected of aiding or abetting the cause of the enemy, may be prevented from pursuing measures injurious to the general weal,*

"*Resolved*, That the Executive authorities of the States of Pennsylvania and Delaware be requested to cause all persons within their respective States notoriously disaffected forthwith to be *apprehended*, disarmed, and secured, till such time as the respective States think they may be released without injury to the common cause."—Jour. Congress, vol. 2, p. 240.

Now it will be at once seen that while this as the previous action looked to the *summary arrest* of persons suspected of disaffection, two distinct considerations were presented therefore,

They were 1st, the fact of a *threatened* invasion ; and 2d, policy and self-preservation.

These it appears were considered as sufficient to sustain the proposed arrests. The notion that such arrests should only be made after an invasion occurs "within the lines of actual combat," finds no support in this preamble and resolution of "the Fathers of the Republic."

But not to linger here. In 1778 these proceedings were had :

"The committee to whom were referred the letters from David Franks, &c., brought in a report, whereupon the letter from David Franks, Esq., Commissary of British Prisoners, to Moses Franks, Esq., of London, enclosed under cover to Capt. Thomas Moore, of Gen. Delancey's regiment, being read,

"*Resolved, That the contents of the said letter manifest a disposition and intentions inimical to the safety and liberty of the United States*, and that Mr. Franks, having endeavored to transmit this letter by stealth within the British lines, has abused the confidence reposed in him by Congress, to exercise within the jurisdiction of these States the office of Commissary to the British prisoners.

" *Resolved*, That Major General Arnold be directed to cause the said David Franks *forthwith to be arrested* and conveyed to the new gaol in this city, there to be confined till the further order of Congress."—Jour. of Con., vol. III, pp. 96, 97.

Mark well these particulars.

1. The action in reference to Mr. Franks was by Congress itself.

2. It was secret, without notice to him.

3. It was, necessarily, without arraignment or trial.

4. His arrest was directed to be made by the military power, by Gen. Arnold, not by a civil officer.

To add to these citations would not be difficult, but it would be useless. For those already given are clear and unanswerable. And surely the denunciation so prevalent in relation to arbitrary arrests should cease to be uttered, *for the Continental Congress approved and authorized them.*

## CHAPTER II.

### IMPRISONMENT.

Strictly, or legally, an "*arrest*" is an "*imprisonment.*" But generally the latter term is extended in its sig-

nification, so as to include or denote confinement in a particular place or building. Or, in other words, it is a continuance and consummation of the arrest. Now, abstractly considered, the one is involved in the other; so that if "the right of seizure of persons" is proper, imprisonment for just causes is also proper.

And in accordance with this abstract view were the acts of the Continental Congress. The following is an interesting example:

"With respect to all such unworthy Americans as, regardless of their duty to their Creator, their country, and their posterity, have taken part with our oppressors, and, influenced by the hope or possession of ignominious rewards, strive to recommend themselves to the bounty of administration, by *misrepresenting and traducing the conduct and principles of the friends of American liberty, and opposing every measure formed for its preservation and security*.

*Resolved*, That it be recommended to the *different assemblies, conventions, and committees, or councils of safety in the United Colonies, by the* MOST SPEEDY *and effectual measures to frustrate the mischievous machinations* and restrain the wicked practices of these men. And it is the opinion of this Congress, that they ought to be disarmed, and the more dangerous among them either KEPT IN SAFE CUSTODY, or bound with sufficient sureties to their good behaviour.

And in order that the said assemblies, conventions, committees, or councils of safety may be enabled with greater ease and facility to carry this resolution into execution—

*Resolved*, That they be *authorized* to call to their aid whatever *continental troops*, stationed in or near their respective colonies, as may be conveniently spared from their more immediate duty; and the commanding officers of such troops are hereby directed to afford the said assemblies, Conventions, Committees, or Councils of Safety all such assistance in executing this resolution as they may require, and which, consistent with the good of the service, may be supplied.—Jour. Con., v. i, p. 22.

The elevated conceptions of patriotism and the scathing rebuke of "unworthy Americans" contained in the introduction to these resolutions, should be deeply pondered. And then, the resolutions, it should be observed, are comprehensive. They included "*all the colonies*." And while the adoption of "the most speedy and effectual measures" against "the tories" were insisted upon, it was specifically recommended that they be "KEPT IN SAFE CUSTODY," i. e. imprisoned. And to accomplish this end, "continental troops" were required to render the Committees of Safety and other similar assemblies every possible assistance.

But not content with this *general* recommendation, Congress became specific, and

*Resolved*, That it be recommended to the convention of the colony of New York, to make effectual provision for detecting, RESTRAINING, and punishing *disaffected* and dangerous persons in that colony, and to prevent all persons from having any intercourse or correspondence with the enemy; and that General Washington afford his aid therein, where necessary.—Jour. Con., vol. 1, p. 373.

Gen. Washington, the commander-in-chief of the army, it seems, was even directed to aid in the enforcement of the measures adopted relative to disaffected and dangerous persons. But even directions so specific as this did not satisfy the wisdom and vigilance of the men of 1775.

On the 1st of December of that year—

"A letter from the committee of Fredericktown, in Maryland, was received and read, containing an account of their having apprehended Major Connolly and his associates, and desiring the advice of Congress with regard to the prisoners."

It was referred to a committee consisting of the "Virginia delegates."

On the 8th of December the committee brought in their report, and it was

"*Resolved*, That the said Allen Cameron, John Smith, and John Connolly be *confined in prison* in Philadelphia at the Continental expense, until the further order of Congress.

"*Ordered*, That the President transmit a copy of the above resolution to the committee of Frederick, and desire them, in pursuance thereof, to send the prisoners under guard to Philadelphia."

On the 3d of January, 1776—

"A letter from the Committee of Frederick, in Maryland, brought by the officer who had the charge of bringing down Connolly and his associates, was laid before Congress and read."

"*Resolved*, That it be recommended to the Committee of Safety of Pennsylvania; to carry into execution the Resolution of Congress for *confining* said Connolly, and his associates *in the gaol* of Philadelphia, and that they take their examination."—Jour. Congress.

The "Committee of Safety" did as requested. But, on 28th March,

"Information being given to Congress that some prisoners in the gaol of Philadelphia have meditated an escape and are near carrying their plan into execution,

"*Resolved*, That the gaoler be directed to to *confine* John Connolly, J. Smith, and Moses Kirkland *in separate apartments and suffer no person to converse with any of them*, without special order of Congress."

And on the 31st of May, it was

"*Resolved*, That John Connolly, John Smith, and Allen Cameron, three of the prisoners confined in the gaol of Philadelphia, who are represented to be in a dangerous state of health, be permitted, for the recovery of their health, to *walk two hours in the day in the yard of the prison, in company with, or under the inspection of at least two of the guards.*"

And on the 12th of December, 1776, when Philadelphia was threatened by the British army, it was

"*Resolved*, That General Putnam be directed to send Dr. John Connolly under guard to Baltimore in Maryland there to be confined."

Now, from these extracts it appears—

1. That the Continental Congress took direct control of Connelly and his associates.

2. That it ordered their imprisonment.

3. That it determined the place of the imprisonment.

4. That it fixed the nature of it—requiring it to be in gaol.

5. That it finally rendered the confinement to be solitary.

6. That it prohibited even conversation with the persons.

7. That the imprisonment was protracted.

8. That impaired health was not regarded as a sufficient reason for their release, or to induce a relaxation of the rigor of their confinement, except only so far as to allow them a brief walk in the prison yard under the vigilance of guards.

In view of such facts as these, how impotent the clamors of 1864 concerning the treatment of "persons of disloyal words and acts!" And how dull and pointless the morbid and plaintive descriptions of the places of their confinement, as dungeons, bastiles, and tombs.* More of true history, a better acquaintance with facts, less of interested perversion of the teachings of the past, and of the sombre shadings of maddened imaginations would be well.

---

*Many of the tories were confined in private houses, a considerable number in jails, some in " Linsbury mines," and others banished from the country.

## CHAPTER III.

### WRIT OF HABEAS CORPUS.

The writ of *habeas corpus* is directly connected with "arrests" and "imprisonment." It can in fact only operate when an individual is in the custody of another, or under his restraint. Recently, much has been advanced from rostrums and through the press relative to its suspension, and factionists have assumed the position that any interference with it is an outrage of no common magnitude upon the privileges of freemen.* And that even amid the schemes of national con-

---

* No reference has been made to *the distinction* which is occasionally drawn between a suspension by the President or by the Congress, because that distinction is not commonly referred to in the speeches, essays, and editorials of the denunciators of the Goverment. It is *any* interference with the writ which they generally oppose.

spirators and the plots and violence of armed rebels, it should remain unrestricted and intact as amid the tranquility and gentleness of hours of peace.

This, however, was not the position of the Continental Congress. For first acting as it did in a twofold capacity—as a legislature and as an executive—it did not at any time use or recognize the writ of *habeas corpus*, or adopt any regulation embracing its principles, or in any manner subject its proceedings, its arbitrary arrests and imprisonments, to any supervisory power. The keenest research cannot produce an instance of its so doing.

Nor were any of its recommendations or requirements addressed to the colonies, relative to the seizure and incarceration of suspected persons, encumbered by any restrictions or conditions. On the contrary, it uniformly proposed decisive and final action, and in harmony with its evident desires, colonies where the writ of *habeas corpus* existed, suspended it.

But this is not all. It is indisputable, that the rights for which the Continental Congress contended, were the rights of British subjects.

But the inviolability of the writ of *habeas corpus*—its perpetual and invariable continuance in full force and vigor—was not one of these rights. No body of men were more familiar with this fact than the Continental Congress. Composed as it was of scholars, historians, and to a considerable extent of lawyers, it knew that the " protective law which gave every man security in time of tranquility " had been suspended again and again in periods of public danger and apprehension. That this had been done in 1696, during the Barclay conspiracy, in the rebellion of 1715, during the Jacobite conspiracy of 1722, at the time of the invasion of the Pretender in 1745, and at other periods, and that hence, by the well established practice of the English government, it was subordinated to the exigencies of the

nation ;"* which to the fullest extent had adopted the maxim, *salus populi suprema est lex*, the welfare of the people is the highest law. To this maxim the Continental Congress confined its practice. and never for a moment intimated that its actions or ultimate purpose could be fettered or impaired by the intervention of any process of technicality or substance. And here it may be properly added that three of its earliest and most valuable papers indicated its views of *the fundamental distinction which exists between periods of war and of peace.*

On the 14th of October, 1774, it agreed upon its " declaration and resolves." Among the latter was the following, viz :

*"Resolve N. C. D.* 9. That the keeping of a standing army in these colonies, IN TIMES OF PEACE, without the consent of the legislature of that colony in which that army is kept, is against law."

On the 21st of October, 1774, it " approved its memorial to the inhabitants of the British colony."

In it this paragraph occurs :

" By an order of the King, the authority of the commander-in-chief, and under him of the brigadier generals, IN TIME OF PEACE, is rendered supreme in all the civil governments in America; and thus an uncontrollable military power is vested in officers, not known to the constitution of these colonies "—Jour. Cong., vol. 1, p. 35.

---

* In 1745, it was stated by the Solicitor General that the writ of *habeas corpus* had been suspended nine times since the " English Revolution ;" and in 1794, Mr. Secretary Dundas made a similar statement.— Parl. Hist xxx. 539; May's Const. Hist. of England, vol. 2, p. 253.

Referring to its suspension in 1689, Macauly in the third volume of his History of England, page thirty-eight, says :

" Extraordinary and irregular vindications of public liberty are sometimes necessary; they are almost always followed by some temporary abridgment of that liberty, and every such abridgment is a fertile and plausible theme for sarcasm and invective." —Page 38, vol. 3.

And in the declaration of independence is this well remembered clause of complaint against George III :

"He has kept among us, IN TIMES OF PEACE, standing armies, without the consent of our legislatures."

From these extracts it is clear that the Continental Congress considered a standing army, and the supremacy of military authority, *only objectionable in times of peace.* Composed as it was of lovers of English liberty to neither, "in times of war," could it or did it except. On the contrary, it appears that in periods of fierce national strife—especially intestine—it regarded both as proper. And during their existence it conceived it judicious to unite the maxims—*salus populi suprema est lex* and *inter arma leges silent*—the laws are silent or disregarded in the midst of arms, the latter of which alone in its operations must have set aside the writ of *habeas corpus.*

And it is thus evinced that the cavils of political place-seekers concerning this great writ and the interference of the military with the civil power, derives no support from the Continental Congress.

## CHAPTER IV.

### SEIZURE OF ARMS.

The seizure of arms in the possession of persons supposed to be in sympathy with the rebellion of the Southern States, has evoked the most acrimonious imprecations and epithets. And to render these potent, "to give them edge and force," article second of the amendment to the Constitution is cited. It reads thus :

ARTICLE II. "A well regulated militia being necessary to the security of a free State, the right of the people to keep and bear arms shall not be infringed."

And with an air of triumph it is asked, does not this give an unrestricted right, an absolute guarantee, to keep and bear arms? The answer is, *it does not.* A careful glance at this article shows *that the security of a free State, of the Government, is the exclusive end for which the right has an existence.* If then it is ascertained that arms are purchased, carried or kept for a purpose or purposes inimical to the Government, they should be promptly seized. *For the right to possess arms to sustain and defend a nation. involves or carries with it no right to possess arms to overthrow a nation.* Treason cannot in this respect claim the prerogative of loyalty, but must be treated as a crime. So the Continental Congress repeatedly determined, as will be manifest to all upon the perusal of this resolution :

"*Resolved,* That it be recommended to the several assemblies, conventions, and committees or councils of safety of the United Colonies, *immediately to cause all pers ns to be disarmed* within their respective colonies, who are notoriously disaffected to the cause of America, or who have not associated, and shall refuse to associate, to defend, by arms these United Colonies, against the hostile attempts of the British fleets and armies, and to apply *the arms taken from such persons* in each respective colony, in the first place to the arming the continental troops raised in said colony, in the next, to the arming such troops as are raised by the colony for its own defence, and the residue to be applied to the arming the associates, etc."—Jour. Cong., vol. 1, p. 285.

This resolution was comprehensive, extending to the "notoriously disaffected," as well as to those who refused to take an active part against the British forces.

Recognizing no distinction between the two classes, it looked to the disarming of both, and the placing of the war-power in the hands of the friends of America.

To this may be appropriately added the following:

The committee appointed to enquire into the grounds of the information respecting a quantity of arms and ammunition being to be procured, report that they have examined into the same, and have received intelligence that a quantity of arms and ammunition and other articles are concealed in Tryon county, in which also there are several tories armed and enlisted in the enemy's service: Whereupon

*Resolved,* That the said committee be directed to communicate this intelligence to Gen. Schuyler, and in the name of the Congress, desire him to take the most speedy and effectual measures *f r securing the said arms and military stores,* and for disarming the said tories and apprehending their chiefs.—Jour. Cong., vol. 1, p. 219.

" *Resolved,* That Gen. Schuyler has proceded in disarming such inhabitants of the county of Tryon, in the colony of New York as were disaffected, and providing for the future tranquility of those parts with fidelity, prudence, and despatch, and at the same time with a proper temper towards that deluded people, and thereby performed a meritorious service."—Jour. Cong. vol. 1, p. 254.

The value of this is unquestionable. It establishes these points: 1. The Continental Congress considered it proper to interfere upon "information" or rumor that arms were about to be procured. 2. Upon ascertaining that arms were concealed and actually in possession, it deemed their seizure by " the most speedy and effectual measures " a solemn duty. 3. It entrusted the immediate performance of the duty to the military power. 4. And when it was quickly and rigorously performed by Gen. Schuyler, he received the approval of Congress.

Examined most carefully, what a sanction of the course of the " powers that be" is this? And how completely it sustains Gen. Carrington in the seizure of arms in Indiana, and Governor Morton in the part he took in that transaction? And what a justification of the order of Gen. Heintzelman, on the 30th of August last, prohibiting the sale, transportation, and delivery of " firearms, powder, or ammunition of any kind for sixty days, within the States of Ohio, Indiana, Illinois, and Michigan, without governmental permission."

Truly, those who object to these military proceedings are only the knights of treason, clad in the garb of the tories of old, and wielding the blunted weapons of " the crown worshippers of the latter part of the eighteenth century."

## CHAPTER V.

### INTERFERENCE WITH CORRESPONDENCE OR SEIZURE OF PRIVATE PAPERS.

The constitutional provision relative to searching houses extends to " papers." The sciolism and factiousness which condemn the one, therefore condemn the other; the patriotism and reasoning which approve the former, justify the latter.

This was the ground upon which the Continental Congress firmly planted itself.

Let a few specimens of its action in this particular be examined.

In 1776, it

" *Resolved,* That a committee of five be appointed to prepare an effectual plan for suppressing the internal enemies of America, and *preventing a communication of intelligence to our other enemies.*

" The members chosen were Mr. S. Adams, Mr. Wythe, Mr. R. H. Lee, Mr. Wilson, and Mr. Ross.—Jour. Cont. Congress, vol. 1, p.  ."

Subsequently, Mr. Chase and Mr. Gerry were added to the committee. Among various reports which it made was the following:

" The Committee appointed to report upon the means of preventing a correspondence with the enemy brought in a report, whereupon Congress came to the following resolution :

"Whereas many letters addressed to individuals of these United States have been lately received in England, through the conveyance of the enemy, and some of them, which have been *under the inspection of Congress, are found to contain ideas insidiously calculated to divide and delude the good people of these States.*

"*Resolved,* That it be, and it is hereby, earnestly recommended to the legislative and Executive authorities of the several States to exercise the utmost care and vigilance, and take the most effectual measures to put a stop to so dangerous and criminal correspondence.

*Resolved,* That the Commander-in-Chief, and the commanders in each and every military department be, and he and they are hereby directed, to carry the measures recommended in the above resolution into the most effectual execution,

*Ordered,* That the foregoing resolutions be forthwith published, and it is recommended to the several printers in the United States to re-publish the same.—Jour. of Cong., vol. II, p. 592."

From the character of the committee, and of this action, it is clear that correspondence with the enemy was considered of the greatest importance.

Hence the recommendation to prevent and suppress it by the use of "the utmost care," and "the most effectual measures." Hence the directions to "the Commander-in-Chief and the commanders in each military department to carry these measures earnestly and fully into execution."

Certainly what was regarded of so much moment by "the wisest and best of statesmen," should not be of "small interest" in this day.

But a more full and complete conception of the manner in which "the Old Congress" proceeded may be obtained from the subjoined extract :

"The Congress taking into consideration the letter from the committee of Baltimore, and the papers enclosed, came to the following resolutions :

"Whereas information has been this day laid before Congress, from which there is great reason to believe that Robert Eden, Esq., Governor of Maryland, has lately carried on a correspondence with the British ministry highly dangerous to the liberties of America.

"*Resolved*, therefore, That the Council of Safety of Maryland be earnestly requested immediately to cause the person *and papers of Governor Eden to be seized and secured, and such of the papers as relate to the American dispute, without delay, conveyed safely to Congress, and that copies of the intercepted letters from the Secretary of State be enclosed to the said Council of Safety.*

"*Resolved,* That the Council of Safety of Maryland be requested to cause the person and *papers* of Alexander Ross to *be immediately seized* and secured, and that the papers be sent safely to Congress.

"And to prevent the said Alexander Ross having any opportunity to escape,

"*Resolved,* That the like request be made to the Committees of Observation for Baltimore and Frederick counties in Maryland, in one of which counties the said Alexander Ross probably now is."

1. It was a governor who was involved in the first part of these proceedings.

2. Not only his person but his *papers* were to be seized.

3. When seized they were to be examined, and those which related to the American dispute were to be conveyed to Congress.

4. It was a private citizen who was embraced in the second resolution.

5. His person and papers were directed to be seized just as the person and papers of a distinguished official.

6. Congress was no respecter of individuals. From it guilt, actual or presumed, received similar and merited treatment.

The papers of no class were regarded as beyond its appropriate grasp, or too sacred for its vision of patriotism.

Not only perfect, but elevated then are the precedents for the "forcible taking" of private letters and telegrams, and "the examination of their contents." And in the judgment of the impartial and loyal of "the times that are upon us," and doubtless in that of the future historian, the epistle of Daniel W. Vorhees, in reference to the criminal papers "discovered and seized" in his office will be distinguished for its want of dignity, its low vindictiveness, and not for the purity of its purpose, or soundness of its positions. It is guilt, not inno-

cence; wrong, not right; which "runs out in words of bitterness and contortion."

## CHAPTER VI.

### DOMICILIARY VISITS, OR SEARCHING OF PRIVATE DWELLINGS.

That the habitation of every one is sacred, is not to be disputed. It is his "castle." Coke was correct in so styling it; and Lord Chatham was correct when he said "it may be a straw-built hut, the wind may enter it, the rain may enter it, but the king cannot."

This is the general legal truth or idea. But if instead of being an asylum for personal ease and enjoyment, an oasis amid the s.ruggles and storms of life, it becomes a haunt of national conspirators, a school of disloyalty, a workshop of traitors, "*the king may enter it.*" He should enter it, because it has ceased to be an abode of quiet and of good, and become one of danger and of evil. Even a *well grounded suspicion* of this perversion or misuse is enough to justify the entry. On these grounds, searching of houses in "unsettled States of the kingdom," has been repeatedly approved in England. Acquainted with this fact, influenced no doubt by it, the Continental Congress did not hesitate on the 26th of August, 1777, to adopt the annexed recommendation:

"*Resolved*, That it be recommended to the Supreme Executive Council of the State of Pennsylvania to cause a diligent search to be made in the houses of all the inhabitants of the city of Philadelphia, who have not manifested their attachment to the American cause, for fire-arms, swords, and bayonets; that the owners of the arms so found be paid for them at an appraised value, and that they be delivered to such of the militia of the State of Pennsylvania who are at present unarmed, and have been called into the field."—Journal Cong., vol. II, p. 240.

This search was to be dilligent "*in the houses*" of all who had failed or neglected to manifest their attachment to the American cause.

The pertinency and decisiveness of this citation render others unnecessary. It may well stand alone in its strength, a stern rebuke to all the utterances of partisan fanaticism concerning the invasion of domestic firesides by those whom they insolently and falsely denounce as "the hirelings of a despot."

But while it is allowed to stand thus and "do its office," it should not be overlooked that it is in exact harmony with the letter and spirit of Article IV of the Amendments of the Constitution, inasmuch as it only prohibits "*unreasonable*" searches. And who except a "northern peace man," a co-operationist with the so-called Southern Confederacy, would pronounce a "search" of a dwelling prostituted to the schemes and plans of the enemies of the Union "unreasonable?" Surely this specimen of the *genus homo*, and he alone, would do it.

## CHAPTER VII.

RESTRAINT UPON TRAVEL, OR INTERFERENCE WITH THE "JOURNEY-
ING" OF SUSPECTED PERSONS.

" The power of locomotion, of changing situation, or moving one's person to whatsoever place one's own inclination may direct," is a part of the personal liberty of every individual. But this, as other parts of that liberty, is not unlimited. It is subject to proper restrictions; and a restriction is eminently proper which impedes, arrests and fetters, a "movement of person," a locomotion of the body designed to "aid the enemies of a government," or to effect its overthrow. Hence this regulation of the " Continental Congress :"

" *Resolved*, That when any persons are desirous of going within the enemy's lines, they shall apply to the Executive powers of the State to which they belong, and if the said Executive powers approve the motives and characters of the persons applying, and shall be of opinion, especially at so critical conjunctures as the present, that no danger will ensue by granting such permission, that they recommend them to the officer commanding the troops next to the enemy who, upon such recommendation, may at his discretion permit the persons to go in."—Journals Continental Congress, vol. III, p. 29.

And hence, too, this regulation :

" *Resolved*, That the Board of War be directed to inquire into the conduct of all strangers of suspicious characters, or whose business is not well known and approved, who may come to the place where Congress sits, and to take care that the public receive no damage by such persons."—Jour. Cont. Congress, vol. 2, p. 437.

And hence these proceedings in harmony with the adopted regulations :

" Whereas, Dr. Parke and one Morton, both of the city of Philadelphia, the former son-in-law, and the latter step-son, of Jas. Pemberton, have presumed to undertake a journey from Philadelphia to Winchester without calling at headquarters, or obtaining* permission from any lawful authority,

" *Resolved*, That the Board of War be directed to cause the said Parke and Morton to be apprehended and confined in prison till further orders."—Jour. of Cong., March 2, 1778, vol. 2, p. 462.

A letter from Fanny Raden was read, praying for leave to go to New York.

" *Resolved*, That leave be not granted." —Journal Continental Congress, volume 3, page 29.

Even woman was restrained from "going where she pleased." " In the days that tried men's souls" she, forgetful of her high endowments, and holy mission on earth, not unfrequently became the emissary of wrong, and the agent of disloyalty. That which she then did, too often she still does. But as the boon of freedom could not *then* be sacrificed to either the proud and insolent demands of the sterner sex or to the schemes and charms of the gentler sex, it cannot *be now*. Appear " mixed up with what nature" it may, treason must be detected, exposed, and deprived of power to harm.

## CHAPTER VIII.

IMPRESSMENT AND USE OF PRIVATE PROPERTY.

Respecting the title to private property there can ordinarily be no dispute. It belongs absolutely to the individual. Yet in periods of " public want or necessity," his control over it must give way to the demands of Government. These demands then become supreme. This is an axiom or principle which permeates every system of civilized law.

The Continental Congress did not hesitate to put it in efficient operation. Consequently on the 10th of December, 1777, it was—

"*Resolved*, That Gen. Washington be informed that Congress have observed with deep concern that the principal supplies for the army under his command, have since the loss of Philadelphia, been drawn from distant quarters, whereby great expense has accrued to the public, the army has been irregularly and scantily supplied, and the established magazines greatly reduced, while large quantities of stock, provisions, and forage, are still remaining in the counties of Philadelphia, Bucks, and Chester, which by the fortune of war may be soon subjected to the power of the enemy.

"*Resolved*, That Gen. Washington be directed to order *every kind of stock and provisions* in the counties above mentioned, which may be beneficial to the army or serviceable to the enemy, *to be taken from all persons* without distinction, leaving such quantities only as he shall judge necessary for the maintenance of their families; the stock and provisions so taken to be removed to places of security under the care of proper persons to be appointed for that purpose.—Jour. Cong., vol. 2, p. 368.

And on the 20th of December, 1777, it was—

"*Resolved*, That it be earnestly recommended to the Legislatures of the United States, forthwith to enact laws appointing suitable persons *to seize and take* for the use of the continental army of the said States, *all woolen cloths, blankets, linens, shoes, stockings, hats, and other necessary articles of clothing* suitable for the army, which may be in the possession of any persons inhabitants of, or residents within their respective States, for the purpose of sale and not for their own private use or family consumption, giving them certificates or receipts for the same, expressing the quantity and quality of the goods, etc.
\* \* \* \* \*
2. That it be further recommended to make provision in the said laws to empower the commissary general of purchases, or any of his deputies, or such other persons as the respective Legislatures may deem expedient, *to seize all stock and every kind*

*of provision* necessary for the army which may have been purchased up or engrossed by any person with a view of selling the same, giving to the person from whom such stock or provisions have been taken, certificates as aforesaid."— Jour. Cont. Cong., vol. 2, p. 379.

The first of these resolutions, it will be observed, extended to "all persons without distinction, resident in the counties of Philadelphia, Bucks, and Chester;" and directed Gen. Washington "*to take from them*" all stock and provisions needed by the army, except so much as he might judge necessary for their families. The direction was positive, and left no option in any respect. The second resolution in its earnest recommendation comprehended all the colonies. It embraced not only "stock" and "provisions" but also "clothing." It proposed that the former should be seized by the commissary general from that "infamous class" who had purchased them up or engrossed them; and that the latter, blankets, linens, shoes, stockings, *et cetera*, in the possession of any one for sale, should be seized for the use of the army and certificates given them.

To the analysis which has been given of this last resolution, should be added an extract from an address which accompanied it, setting forth the grounds for the employment of the means it included. Here it is:

"It is with deep concern that Congress, after having for some time contemplated in painful silence the mischiefs which threatened this extended continent from the growing avarice of the times, feel themselves constrained to recommend measures which the virtue of all classes of men rendered not long since unnecessary, and which a scrupulous regard for security of property to every citizen of these States has hitherto restrained from adopting. But, unhappy the case of America! laws unworthy the character of infant republics *are become necessary to supply the defect of public virtue*, AND TO CORRECT THE VICES OF SOME OF HER SONS; AND SHE IS CALLED UPON BY THE GRAND PRINCIPLE OF SELF-PRESERVATION, TO GUARD AGAINST THE PARRICIDE OF THOSE WHOM SHE HAS FOSTERED IN HER OWN BOSOM."

That the considerations which it presents "the defect of public virtue, viz., growing, prevalent political vices, and the grand principle of self-preservation," would sustain in the pending crisis similar measures to a far greater extent than they have been employed, may be safely affirmed. Nevertheless, if this were done, what cries of censure, fierce and loud as the shrieks of aroused demons, would break forth from Mozart and Tammany Halls, and all kindred dens! But all this would be of little consequence; for not even an angel's emotions or deeds could secure their approval.

## CHAPTER IX.

### CONFISCATION OF THE PROPERTY, REAL AND PERSONAL, OF TORIES.

The indignation of not a few has been "stirred to its lowest depths" because the Government has seen fit to confiscate the property of "rebels in arms" and their "aiders and abettors."

This has been represented as one of extreme severity, and as "contrary to the civilization of all the past."

And the President, in neatly printed and artfully prepared pamphlets, has been charged with "treasonable intent, purpose, and designs, in having approved, indorsed, and partially carried into execution the unconstitutional act of Congress known as the Confiscation Bill."

To all this a most complete refutation is found in this proceeding, viz:

Congress resumed the consideration of the report of the committee on the letter from S. Hopkins, Esq., &c.: Whereupon

"*Resolved*, That it be earnestly recommended to the several States, as soon as may be, TO CONFISCATE AND MAKE SALE OF ALL THE REAL AND PERSONAL ESTATE THEREIN of such of their inhabitants and other persons who have FORFEITED the same, and the right to the protection of their respective, and to invest the money arising from the sales in continental loan-office certificates, to be appropriated in such manner as the respective States shall hereafter direct."— Jour. Cont. Cong., Nov. 27, 1777, vol 2, p. 352.

Let it be particularly noted that the recommendation extended not only to *all personal* but also to *all real estate.*

The Continental Congress, in the clearest manner, approved of the confiscation of both.

"Where the fathers trod, the sons should not hesitate to go."

---

* This recommendation was not *brutum fulmum.* It lead to extensive confiscation. In North Carolina, sixty-five individuals and four mercantile firms were deprived of their estates, "INCLUDING NEGROES." In South Carolina, at least 157. In New Hampshire, Pennsylvania, New York, and other States, the confiscation amounted to several hundred.

## CHAPTER X.

### INTERFERENCE WITH ELECTIONS.

The purity of elections is of no ordinary value. All concede this, none deny it. The Continental Congress admitted it. But it was far from believing or maintaining that Government should have no control over the ballot box. It believed and maintained the very opposite. It approved of "the polls" being surrounded with safeguards and tests of feelings and "opinions." It went even beyond this, as the subjoined selection from its "minutes" of the 3d of January, 1776, demonstrates:

"The Committee on the State of New York brought in a further report, which being taken into consideration was agreed to as follows:

"Whereas a majority of the inhabitants of Queen's county, in the Colony of New

York, being incapable of resolving to live and die freemen, and being more disposed to quit their liberties than part with the little portion of their property necessary to defend them, *have deserted the American cause by refusing to send deputies as usual to the convention of that col ny*, and avowing by a public declaration, an unmanly design of remaining inactive spectators to the present contest, vainly flattering themselves, perhaps, that should Providence declare for our enemies they may purchase their mercy and favor at an easy rate; and, on the other hand, if the war should terminate in favor of America, that then they may enjoy, without expense of blood or treasure, all the blessings resulting from that liberty which they, in the day of trial, had abandoned, and in defence of which many of their more virtuous neighbors and countrymen had nobly died; and although the want of public spirit, observable in these men, rather excites pity than alarm, there being little danger to apprehend either from their powers or example, yet it being reasonable that those who refuse to defend their country should be excluded from its protection, and prevented from doing it injury:

"*Resolved*, That all such persons in Queen's county aforesaid *as voted against sending deputies to the present convention* of New York, and named in a list of delinquents in Queen's county, published by the convention of New York, *be put out of the protection of the United Colonies, and that all trade and intercourse with them cease;* that none of the inhabitants of that county be permitted to travel or abide in any part of these United Colonies, out of their said county, without a certificate from the Convention, or Committee of Safety of the colony of New York, setting forth that such inhabitant is a friend of the American cause, *and not of the number of those who voted against sending deputies to the said convention*, and that such of the said inhabitants as shall be found out of the said county, without such certificate, be apprehended and imprisoned three months:

*Resolved*, That no attorney or lawyer ought to commence, prosecute, or defend, any action at law, of any kind, for any of the said inhabitants of Queen's county who voted against sending deputies to the Convention, as aforesaid, and such attorney or lawyer as shall contravene this resolution are enemies to the American cause, and ought to be treated accordingly:

"*Resolved*, That the Convention or committee of safety of the Colony of New York be requested to continue publishing for a month, in all their gazettes or newspapers, the names of all such inhabitants of Queen's county as voted against sending

deputies; and to give certificates in the manner before recommended, to such others of the said inhabitants as are friends to American liberty.

"And it is recommended to all conventions, committees of safety, and others, *to be diligent* in executing the above resolutions.

"*Resolved*, That Col. Nathaniel Heard, of Woodbridge, in the Colony of New Jersey, taking with him five or six hundred minute men under discreet officers, do march to the western part of Queen's county, and that Col. Waterbury, of Stanford, in the Colony of Connecticut, with like number of minute men march to the eastern side of said county; that they confer together and endeavor to enter the said county on one day; *that they proceed to disarm every person in the said county who voted against sending deputies to the said convention, and cause them to deelivr up their arms and ammunition on oath, and that they take and confine in safe custody till further orders, all such as refuse compliance.*

"That they apprehend and secure till further orders, the persons named as principal men among the disaffected in the said county, in a summons for their appearance before the convention of New York, issued the 12th of December last, viz:

*Of Jamaica Township*—Capt. Benjamin Whitehead, Charles Arden, Joseph French, Esq., Johannes Polhemus.

*Newtown*—Nathaniel Moor, John Moor, Sen., Samuel Hallet, John Moor, Jun., Wm. Weyman, John Shoals, Jeromus Rapalje.

*Flushing*—John Willet.

*Hamstead*—Justice Gilbert Van Wyck, Daniel Kissam, Esq., of Cowneck; Captain Jacob Mott, Thomas Cornbill of Rockaway, Gabriel G. Ludlow, Richard Hewlet, Capt. Charles Hicks, Dr. Samuel Martin, Justice Samuel Clowes.

*Oyster Bay*—Justice Thomas Smith of Hog Island, Justice John Hewlet, Captain George Weeks, Dr. David Brooks, Justice John Townsend.

"And all such other persons who shall be found in arms, *or who shall oppose the carrying the resolutions into effect*, as the said Col. Heard or Col. Waterbury may think prudent to detain.

"*Resolved*, That it be recommended to the said Col. Heard and Col. Waterbury to execute the business entrusted to them by the foregoing resolutions, *with all possible despatch, secrecy, order, and humanity.*—Vol. 1, pp. 224, 225, Jour. Cont. Congress.

"*Resolved*, That the delegates of New Jersey and Connecticut be directed to take the necessary steps for carrying into execution the resolutions of Congress passed on Wednesday last, respecting the inhabitants of Queen's county.—Friday, Jan. 5, 1776, vol. 1, p. 227, Jour. Cont. Congress.

Let the eye and the mind linger over these extracts and note these salient particulars. 1. The indignation and scorn of the preamble. In these respects no paper of the Congress surpassed it. 2. This indignation and scorn was called forth by the fact that a majority of the inhabitants voted against sending delegates to the New York Convention of Independence. 3. The Congress treated this refusal, or determination with regard to delegates, as grave offense against "the United Colonies." 4. So regarding it, it interfered with the election, or, more correctly, with the persons, in a section of New York, who voted contrary to its desires or purposes. 5. It required those who so voted to "be put out of protection," excluded from "trade and intercourse," prevented from travel or residence in any of the Colonies, published and imprisoned. 6. It called upon not "the civil but martial arm" to arrest, disarm, etc., all such persons, and to do so with all possible despatch, secrecy, etc. 7. It deprived them of the assistance of counsel learned in the law, by rendering it odious and censurable to appear for them in any proceeding.

Compared with these provisions how mild the orders of Gen. Schenck and others in relation to the Maryland election, and of Gen. Burnside and others respecting the Kentucky elec-

tions.* And yet with what rare vindictiveness, and with what base scurrility have they been assailed! *Only, however, let it be remembered, that by means less stringent and less severe, they aimed at the same end as the Continental Congress, i. e., to prevent by judicious means such a use of the elective franchise " by evil disposed persons," as would " aid the armed enemies of the country," and defeat the will of its friends, and their conduct will have ample justification.*

Higher, stronger justification none except the captious and the disloyal would demand.

* The order of Gen. Schenck was intended, as it states, to prevent persons who had "been engaged in rebellion against the lawful Government," etc., from "embarrassing the election," and directed provost marshals and other military officers to arrest *such* persons, and to *support* the judges of the election in requiring an oath of allegiance to the United States.

The order of Gen. Burnside was of a similar import. It recites the fact that Kentucky was "invaded by a rebel force with the avowed purpose of overawing the judges of the election, of intimidating the loyal voters, and forcing the election of disloyal candidates, and that the military force only could defeat the attempt; it was therefore required" to aid the constituted authorities of the State in support of the laws and purity of suffrage.—McPherson's Political History, pp. 309, 313.

## CHAPTER XI.

### Speculation in Continental Money or Depreciating Public Credit.

The views and action of the Continental Congress relative to the circulating medium issued by its order, and the integrity of the national finances, were of the most decided character. That they were will be fully seen from these extracts :

"Whereas the Continental money *ought to be supported* at the full value expressed in the respective bills by the inhabitants of these States, for whose benefit they were issued, and who stand bound to redeem the same according to the like value; and the pernicious artifices of the enemies of American liberty to impair the credit of the said bills by raising the nominal value of gold and silver, or any other species of money whatsoever, *ought to be guarded against and prevented :*

"*Resolved*, That all bills of credit, emitted

by authority of Congress, ought to pass current in all payments, trade, and dealings, in these States, *and be deemed in value equal to the same nominal sums in Spanish milled dollars ;* and that whosoever shall offer, ask, or receive more in the said bills for any gold or silver coins, bullion, or any other species of money whatsoever, than the nominal sum or amount thereof in Spanish milled dollars, or more, in the said bills, for any lands, houses, goods, or commodities whatsoever, than the same could be purchased at of the same person or persons in gold, silver, or any other species of money whatsoever ; or shall offer to sell any goods or commodities for gold or silver coins, or any other species of money whatsoever, and refuse to sell the same for the said continental bills, *every such person ought to be deemed an enemy to the liberties of these United States, and to forfeit the value of the money so exchanged, or house, land, or commodity so sold or offered for sale.* And it is recommended to the legislatures of the respective States, to enact laws inflicting such forfeitures and other penalties on offenders as aforesaid, as will prevent such *pernicious practices :*

" That it be recommended to the legislatures of the United States to pass laws to make the bills of credit, issued by the Congress, a lawful tender in payments of public and private debts ; *and a refusal thereof an extinguishment of such debts ;* that debts payable in sterling money be discharged with continental dollars, at the rate of 4s 6d sterling per dollar ; and that in discharge of all other debts and contracts, continental dollars pass at the rate fixed by the respective States, for the value of Spanish milled dollars."—Jour. Cont. Cong., vol. 2, p. 12.

" *Resolved,* That the council of safety of Pennsylvania be requested to take the most rigorous and speedy measures for *punishing all such as refuse continental currency ;* and that the General be directed to give all necessary aid to the council of safety, for carrying their measures on this subject into effectual execution."—Jour. Cont. Cong. vol. 1, p. 585.

Extended comments on these extracts are not required. They show fully " the position of the ancient lovers of liberty " with regard to " their promises to pay," or the money of the Revolutionary era. They insisted that it should be supported and received in value " as equal to gold and silver." And they urged with " great earnestness " that all attempts to prevent this—to depreciate the continental currency—should be considered as an offence to be punished by forfeiture of property, extinguishment of debts, and otherwise. In fact, the Continental Congress considered " the money-changers " of their day—the regular speculators in the precious metals—as unworthy a place in the " temple of liberty." To a great extent they are still so. And if not a few brokers of Wall street—the gamblers in Government stocks and notes—were arrested in their peculations and depreciations by proper penal enactments, it would be well. If base and mercenary in their purpose, *they will* cripple the arm of the nation as it deals out its blows upon the monster of rebellion, why should they not by more than " knotted scourges " be expelled from the heritage of freedom ? Certain it is " gold bills," laws regulating and restraining " traffic in national funds," had the support of the old Congress.

## CHAPTER XII.

### RELIGION AND POLITICS.

The true relation of religion to civil government, or as it is more commonly called, of " the pulpit to politics," is a question of no common interest and importance, and the discussion of this theme *in extenso,* might not be inappropriate. But this is not now *required.* It will be sufficient to show in the first place, that the Continental Congress did not consider that there was a wide and impassible gulf between Christianity and the science of government, and that civil affairs were " too profane, too vile," to be touched by piety, or introduced into the temples of God ; and in the second place, that it *neither approved nor tolerated* the assumption that "under the guise of religion and sheltered by the sanctities of the church," treason might utter its teachings, mumble or articulate its prayers, and accomplish its nefarious purposes.

As respects the first of these points, the proceeding of May 8th, 1778, may be cited:

"The committee appointed to prepare an address to the inhabitants of the United States of America, brought in a draught which was taken into consideration, and sundry amendments being made therein, was agreed to: Therefore it was
"*Resolved*, That it be recommended to *ministers of the gospel* of all denominations, *to read or cause to be read* immediately after divine service, the *above address* to the inhabitants of the United States of America, *in their respective churches and chapels* and other places of religious worship."—Jour. Cont. Cong., vol. 2, pp. 542, 545.

The address, it will be remarked, "was to be read *in* the churches and chapels by the ministers of the gospel," etc. Neither the one nor the other was regarded as unbecoming. The Congress thus declared in the most unequivocal manner not only that "the temple and the priest at its altar," were not degraded by an association with politics, but that it was proper that their influence should be directly exerted "in behalf of the struggle for independence."
And the fact should not be omitted that this address referred, among other subjects, to those of battle and victory, territory and soil, food and taxation, clothing and money; and that it contained a pungent and reproachful denunciation of "the enemies which America had nourished in her bosom."
As to the second point, one of numerous cases may be given.* It is this:

"A petition from the Rev. Mr. Daniel Batwell was read, setting forth 'that by means of his confinement, he is languishing under a dangerous disorder,' and praying 'to be enlarged on parole, or on giving security, or both, an indulgence which he requests for the sake of his private affairs and the re-establishment of his health.' Also, a certificate from Dr. Henry was read, testifying 'that the petitioner labors under a complication of disorders, and that clear air and gentle exercise are absolutely necessary for his recovery:'
"Whereupon, it was *moved*, 'That the petitioner be allowed to go to his farm, giving his parole *to hold no correspondence with the enemies* of the United States, *nor to do anything whatever to the prejudice of the American cause*, there to remain till further orders.
So it passed in the *negative*.
"*Resolved*, That in the opinion of Congress, the Rev. Mr. Batwell should *be discharged from confinement on taking an oath of allegiance* to the State of Pennsylvania, or on his refusal, that he should be allowed to go with his family into the city of Philadelphia."—Jour. Cont. Cong., Dec. 27, 1777, vol. 2, p. 385.

Mr. Batwell, wearing a sacerdotal robe "consecrated to holy orders," had been an active partisan of the king, and was "apprehended and committed to the York jail in the province of Pennsylvania." Nor could his "complicated disorders" nor his "private affairs" secure his release only upon the condition of his taking an oath of allegiance. Otherwise he was required to remain a prisoner of State, in Philadelphia.
Such are the responses which the Continental Congress furnishes to those who would separate the nation's struggle for existence and perpetuity from the purity and sacredness of Christianity, who would hush into silence all reference to "politics in the pulpit," and who would so pervert the "rights of conscience and the free exercise of religion" as to allow her ministers to become with impunity the secret promoters or public agents of treason.

---

* About one hundred "ministers of the Gospel" were distinguished for disloyalty. Several of them were arrested and punished, not for "overt acts," but for speaking or writing against the Colonial authorities. Certain it is that the Revolutionary fathers did not confound "*liberty* of speech" with "*licentiousness* of speech," nor tolerate, even in the pulpit, "utterances tending to prevent the attainment of independence."

# CHAPTER XIII.

## RETALIATION FOR CRUELTIES TO PRISONERS.

War has its laws as well as peace. Among them is this:

"A prisoner of war is subject to no punishment for being a public enemy, nor is any revenge wreaked upon him by the intentional infliction of any suffering, or disgrace, by cruel imprisonment, want of food, by mutilation, death, or any other barbarity."

Forgetful or regardless of this rule, attempting to put back the beneficent march of the centuries, "the Southern Confederacy" has dragged up the violent maxims and more than ferocious practices of the ancients, and usages of the Gothic ages, and inflicted the most attrocious wrongs and cruelties upon prisoners of war. On various occasions she has not hesitated to confine them in most loathsome dungeons or malarious enclosures—to deprive them of common food and drink—to place them in localities exposed to the fire of "Union guns," and to bayonet, sabre, and shoot them after their surrender. To prevent this barbarous conduct, the authorities of the United States have, in a few instances, and to a very limited extent, resorted to retaliation. And yet for doing so, they have become the special subjects of partisan scurrility.

Justified, however, as they have been in this, as in other respects, by the rules and practice of all civilized nations, at the same time they have been sustained by "the Old Congress." Of the correctness of this assertion, the following citation from its proceedings furnishes ample proof.

Mr. Smith, having previously obtained the general consent of the House, moved the following resolutions:

Whereas it hath been represented to Congress that the enemy, at the time of, and since their landing in Virginia, have perpetrated the most unnecessary, wanton, and outrageous barbarities on divers of the citizens of that State, as well as on several of the subjects of his most Christian majesty residing therein; deliberately putting many of them to death in cool blood, after they had surrendered, abusing women, and desolating the country with fire:

*Resolved,* That the Governor of Virginia be requested to cause diligent inquiry to be made into the truth of the above representations, and to transmit to Congress the evidence he may collect on the subject.

*Resolved, That Congress will retaliate for cruelties and violations of the law of nations,* committed in these States against the subjects of his most Christian majesty, in like manner and measure as if committed against citizens of the said States; and that the protection of Congress shall be, on all occasions, equally extended to both."—Journals of Cont. Congress, vol. iii, p. 288.

# CHAPTER XIV.

## EXCLUSION OF DISLOYAL OR DISAFFECTED PERSONS FROM OFFICIAL POSITIONS.

In the United States, no one has an original or inherent claim to official position. Office, therefore, while it may be solicited as a favor, cannot be demanded as a right.

And no man can be said "to suffer a wrong" because of exclusion from any place of "honor, profit, or trust."

But this is not all. Those entrusted with the administration of the affairs of the nation are fully justifiable in excluding and repelling from its departments all whose principles or designs are in any respect antagonistic to its purpose and principles.

So the Continental Congress believed, and in accordance with its belief were its proceedings. Hence on the 26th of December, 1777, it was—

"*Resolved*, That a committee of three be appointed to devise *effectual means* to prevent persons *disaffected to the interest of the United States, from being employed in any of the important offices thereof;* the members chosen, Mr. Roberdeau, Mr. Clark, and Mr. Ellery."—Jour. Cont. Cong., vol. 2, p. 484.

And on the 29th of January, 1778, it was

*Ordered*, That the President write to the Governor of Virginia, and inform him of this resolution. Congress took into consideration the report of the committee appointed to devise *effectual means to prevent persons disaffected to the interest of the United States*, from being employed in any of the important offices thereof. — Jour. Cont. Cong., vol. 2, pp. 422 and 423.

It will at once be perceived that the employment of "*disaffected persons*" in offices, was considered highly objectionable, so much so as to call for the appointment of a committee to devise "*effectual means*" to prevent the evil. And as far as possible *it was prevented*.

The investigation of "the War Committee," and as it is familiarly called "the Potter Committee," and the dismissal of civilians and of "military chieftains" whose loyalty was conditional or uncertain, and whose opinions and principles were not in harmony with those of the Administration, are then in all respects fully sustained.

Indeed, it is only to be regretted that the investigations have not been more searching and the removals more numerous.

"*No nation, no organization, no party, can be safe in the hands of either its enemies or lukewarm friends. And a man in position in this crisis of our country should not only be loyal, but should be above suspicion.*"

Let these sentiments be more fully carried out and fewer "secrets of State" will be prematurely disclosed, and "rebels in arms" will obtain less of valuable information than heretofore. It is true that if this be done the cry of "*proscription for opinions sake*" may increase in volume as well as bitterness, but no one should be deterred from the performance of duty by "railing accusations," especially if they proceed from those who while "banqueting at the table of the nation, are without deep sympathy with her struggles and unqualified attachment to her interests."

By the patriots of old, such characters would have been hurled "from place," as Milton's Satan was hurled from Heaven.

## CHAPTER XV.

### Requirement of Test Oaths.

Oaths are styled by Dr. Cudworth, in his Intellectual System, "a necessary vinculum of society."

And Story, in his Commentaries, refers to an oath as "a suitable pledge of fidelity and responsibility to" one's country, creating upon the "conscience a deep sense of duty, by an appeal, at once in the presence of God and man to the most sacred and solemn sanctions which can operate upon the human mind."

The power of this "vinculum"—this obligation—was invoked by the first Congress.

It therefore

*Resolved*, That *every officer* who holds, or shall hereafter hold *a commission or office* from Congress, shall take and subscribe the following oath or affirmation:

"I, ————, do acknowledge the United States of America to be *free*, independent, and sovereign States, and declare that the people thereof owe no allegiance or obedience to George the Third, king of Great

Britain; and I renounce, refuse, and abjure any allegiance or obedience to him; and I do swear, (or affirm,) that I will, to the utmost of my power, support, maintain and defend the said United States against the said King George the Third, and his heirs and successors, and his and their *abettors, assistants, and adherents*, and will serve the said United States in the office of ——, which I now hold, with fidelity, according to the best of my skill and understanding, so help me God."—Jour. Cong., Feb. 3, 1778, vol. 2, pp. 127, 128.

This obligation was absolute in its terms. It contained not only an acknowledgment of the freedom, independence, and sovereignty of the United States, but a renunciation of any allegiance to "George the Third." It, moreover, required not only *maintenance and defence of "the States"* against the king, and his heirs or successors, but against all who ASSISTED OR ADHERED TO HIM. It bound directly to military service, to active operations against each of these classes.

But the oaths exacted extended beyond this. Here is an instance which evinces the mode in which they were "*run out* so as to cover the most minute enactments," and to operate as "*a test of loyalty in commerce and traffic :*"

"*Resolved*, That it be earnestly recommended to the legislative and executive authorities of 'the respective States, not to grant any exemption from embargo to any vessels whatever, unless, in addition to the former security recommended, the persons applying for the same, comply with the following stipulations, to wit :

"That the shipper or shippers of the cargo solemnly *make oath*, that no part of the flour or grain proposed to be shipped has been purchased or contracted for since the 10th of October, 1778 : *That the shipper and every man on board of the said vessels, whether seamen or passengers, solemnly swear that they will not, directly or indirectly, be privy to or concerned in any measure whatsoever, which may tend to defeat the arrival of the vessel at some safe port in one of the eastern States ; but that they will, without any deception, mental reservation or equivocation whatever, take every measure to carry into effect the intention of the license granted.*"—Jour. Cont. Cong., vol. 3, p. 78.

This oath, it will be observed, in-cluded besides the shippers, *the seamen and passengers, and required all of them to co-operate in running the vessel into a safe Colonial port.*

Or in other words, to aid the Government in the maintenance of its embargo act of June 8, 1778, prohibiting the exportation of wheat, flour, etc., except in so far as "departures" from its provisions were particularly authorized.

It is thus shown, that in the judgment of the Congress, it was proper "to impose a test or governmental oath" upon persons disconnected with civil or military positions, and who were chiefly engaged in industrial avocations or pursuits. That which it considered should be done in the infancy of the nation—while in fact it was in a chrysalis condition—should not be neglected in its matured life.

That *life* should be maintained and perpetuated among other modes, by the ramification of "test oaths" into all the departments of society—mechanical, mercantile, agricultural, and professional, whenever "the proper authorities" may deem it expedient or necessary. Nor can the right to exact them be in the least affected by the clamors of traitors in masquerade, or the grave denunciations of that class who can discover neither virtue nor principle with those who do not swell the numbers of their ranks or advance their aspirations for "rule and plunder," and who appear determined "to lie down those with whom they cannot cope on a fair field."

———o———

To increase these illustrative citations or "precedents," would only require time and space. Throughout, the chief difficulty has been that of "judicious selection from a mass of pertinent material," all of which is in a high degree interesting and valuable.

But an accumulation of citations cannot fairly be demanded. With a plainness which stupidity cannot do otherwise than comprehend and a conclusiveness which intellectual subtlety

24

cannot assail, it has been established that *the Continental Congress recommended, required, or justified measures of the most stringent nature against those who were either indifferent to " the struggle for independence," or refused or neglected to " take an active part in its deliberations and deeds," or who assisted, directly or indirectly, " the British Parliament, Crown, or arms,"* and that these measures entirely harmonize with those which the Administration of Mr. Lincoln has employed in the suppression of the unprovoked rebellion, which has convulsed and desolated our land.

IF, THEN, HE HAS ERRED, THE CONTINENTAL CONGRESS ERRED.

IF THE MEANS WHICH HE HAS EMPLOYED TO DEFEND AND PRESERVE THE NATION HAVE BEEN WRONG, THE MEANS WHICH THE CONTINENTAL CONGRESS EMPLOYED FOR ITS FORMATION WERE WRONG.

TO DENOUNCE THE ONE, IS TO DENOUNCE THE OTHER. TO APPROVE THE ONE IS TO APPROVE THE OTHER.

LET NOT THESE IMPORTANT TRUTHS BE FORGOTTEN.

# PART II.

The political system of the Colonies during the Revolutionary era was to some extent anomalous.

The Continental Congress, however, in its distinctive features or powers, resembled the present Congress of the Union.

Rieves, in his Life of Madison, (vol. I, pp. 211, 212,) refers to it as the "General Congress," and says:

"It exercised the widest possible range of political functions, legislative, executive, and even judicial. It possessed the power of peace and war; conducted foreign negotiations; received ambassadors and ministers; appointed diplomatic agents of its own, as well as all civil and military officers of the higher grades employed in the service of the United States; exercised a general superintendence and control over the operations of the war; determined the amount and description of the land and naval forces to be raised by the States; fixed the sums of money to be contributed by them for the common defence and other purposes, and appropriated the same; and in short was charged, theoretically at least, with the general interests of the Confederacy in whatever concerned its collective action without, or the preservation of harmony within."

Such were the functions of the body whose opinions and practice relative to those who were passively or actively inimical to the struggle for independence, have, to an important extent, been produced.

The facts that its members were chosen or elected from the several Colonies at different periods, and that they were not infrequently changed, creates a strong presumption that it fairly represented their views and policy. This presumption would be fully sustained by an elaborate examination of the proceedings and determination of their legislative and executive departments.

But within prescribed limits no such examination can be attempted. It will not be possible to refer, even in the most general mode, to the records or proceedings of the thirteen Colonies; and, hence, only brief and condensed extracts from those of New York, Pennsylvania, and Maryland, will be given. The comments must necessarily be few and concise. For the purpose of perspicuity, the topical arrangements already adopted will be mainly pursued.*

---

* A few of the chapters in Part I, relate to matters over which the Continental Congress had exclusive control. No corresponding chapters will be found in this part; but the omissions will be supplied by the introduction of subjects which received more attention from "the State assemblies than from the General Congress."

## NEW YORK.

In the life of John Jay, vol. 1, p. 41, it is said, "of all the colonies, New York was probably the least unanimous in the assertion and defence of the principles of the revolution."

These facts however only intensified the zeal and invigorated the efforts of the friends of freedom, and as early as May 22d, 1775, delegates previously elected, met and organized "to consider and execute such measures as might be essential to the common safety." This organization was continued with unimportant modifications during nearly two years. It appointed various committees, including "A Committee of Safety," composed of persons selected from its own number to which it entrusted to a large extent "the management of affairs. When at length it dissolved itself, it left the affairs of the government principally in the hands of a Council of this character. It was succeeded by the Legislature, created under the constitution adopted on the 20   April, 1777. It will be from the       of these several assemblies that extracts will be given.

## CHAPTER I.

### ARBITRARY ARRESTS.

These were numerous. Here are some of the directions or regulations concerning them:

1. "The report of the Committee, for that purpose, on the danger to which this colony is exposed from the intestine enemies, and the ways and means necessary to be taken to guard against those dangers," was made through Mr. Alsop, their chairman,—"read and approved of."

It recited the resolution of the Continental Congress of 6th October, 1776.

And among other things proposed the following, which was adopted, viz:

"That it be recommended to all the general county committees in the several *counties* of this colony to APPREHEND* all persons holding military commissions under the King of Great Britain; and also all such persons holding civil offices under the said or King, being *possessed of influence** in their respective counties as are *suspected* of holding principles inimical to the said united colonies; and, after they shall have been apprehended, to deal with them in such manner as is prescribed," &c.—New York Provincial Congress, American Archives, IV Series, vol. vi, p. 1332.

In addition to other classes, those *possessed of influence* were to be apprehended, and simply because *suspected* of *holding principles* inimical to the colonies. Corresponding acts were not required in order to authorize arrests.

2. "Whereas, The Secret Committee (*i. e.* Messrs. Livingston, Morris, and Jay) appointed the 17th instant have represented to this Congress that they have discovered certain *dangerous persons* who ought to be arrested;

"*Resolved*, That the said Committee, or any two of them, do cause such persons to *be apprehended* and secured *in such a manner* as they may think *most prudent*, and that they have authority either to employ the militia or obtain detachments of Continental troops from the Commander-in-Chief for that purpose, and that they be so far absolved from their oaths of secresy as may be necessary thereto."—*Ibid*, p. 1419.

By this arrests were directed in whatever mode the "Secret Committee" might deem prudent. It was not required in making them to proceed "according to the forms and processes of the criminal books." And besides it was empowered to employ "military force" general or local.

Here is a peculiar case:

"Congress being informed that Captain John Johnson had it in his power to appre-hend a negro of Colonel Edmund Fanning who had been used to keep up a communication with the ships of war, and the ship on board of which Gov. Tryon resides,

"*Ordered*, *That Captain Johnson be requested to cause the said negro to *be apprehended*, and put into safe custody until further orders."—*Ibid.*, 1,365.

Slavery then existed in New York. Arrests it appears were authorized of the slave without consultation with the "owner" or without his permission.

---

* These county committees were, on the 15th of May, 1776, authorized by the Congress to apprehend in whatever way they might think proper dangerous persons, &c.

*This is the mode in which Congress effected arrests, *i. e.*, by direction to an appropriate civilian or military officer. The Committee of Safety pursued the same course, or used an order in the nature of a *general warrant.*

# CHAPTER II.

## IMPRISONMENT.

As arrests were numerous, so were imprisonments.* Of the many instances which might be cited, these will be sufficient:

1. On the 5th of June, 1776, Congress adopted this preamble :

"Whereas there is in this Colony divers persons who, by reason of their holding offices from the king of Great Britain, from their having neglected or refused to associate with their fellow citizens for the defence of their common rights, from their having never manifested by their conduct a zeal for and attachment to the American cause, or from their having maintained an equivocal neutrality, have been considered by their countrymen in a suspicious light, whereby it hath become necessary as well for the safety as for the satisfaction of the people, who in times so dangerous and critical are naturally led to consider those as their enemies who withhold from them their aid and influence."

In a resolution it then named persons of the classes referred to, and directed that they " and all such others as the Committee of Safety might think proper to bring before it by summons or arrest should show cause, if any they had, why they should be considered as friends to the American cause, and in the event of it being determined that they were not, it provided :

"That such of them as may be *men of influence* in the neighborhood of the place of their present residence, *be removed* to such place in this or a neighboring Colony as will deprive them of an opportunity of exerting that influence to the prejudice of the American cause, and respectively bound by their parole, or word of honor, or other security, at the discretion of the said committee, neither directly or indirectly to oppose or contravene *the measures of the Continental Congress*, or the Congress of this Colony, and to abide in the place and within the limits to be assigned them till the further

order of the present or future Provincial Congress, or Continental Congress; and in case they shall refuse to give such parole, or other security, to commit them to safe custody."—American Archives, 4th series, vol. VI, pp. 1368-9-70.

This demands special attention. It was *neutrality, inactivity, indifference* to the American cause which were to constitute the chief considerations for the contemplated arrests. It was required that the parties arrested should prove their attachment to that cause. If they failed to do so they were to be sent out of New York and to be kept within assigned limits in an adjacent colony, or else imprisoned—committed to safe custody.*

2. On the 27th July, 1776, it was

"*Resolved*, that William Sutton (of Long Island) be immediately sent under safe and proper guard, at his own expense, to the jail of Philadelphia, in the State of Pennsylvania; that he subsist himself  *   * *   * American Arch., 5th sec., vol. 1, pp. 1,454-55."

It will be observed that Mr. Sutton besides being removed to the Philadelphia jail was compelled to support himself; nor was the plea of ill health of any avail in securing his release.

3. On the 14th August, 1776, a committee examined Elizabeth Hicks, "a young lady of Roxaway," who had received and delivered a letter to Joshua Mills. The examination and her conduct were unsatisfactory and the Provincial Convention

"Ordered, that the said Elizabeth Hicks be apprehended and kept in safe custody until she discover on oath (or affirmation, if she is one of the people called Quakers,) from whom she received the said paper, or

---

* Some of the prisoners were confined in "Forts Montgomery and Constitution."—*American Archives, 4th Sec., vol. 6th p.* 1358.

* Among the "prisoners of State" was David Mathews, Mayor of New York. So closely was he guarded "that even on private business he could not be spoken to only in presence of a member of the Provincial Congress."—*Ibid*, 1440.

subscribe a declaration on her oath or affirmation that she does not know, or has not any reason to suspect, of whom she received the same; and if the said Elizabeth Hicks shall refuse to make such discovery, or refuse to make and subscribe such declaration on oath or affirmation as aforesaid, that she be confined in the jail of Queen's county, there to remain until she make discovery, or such declaration as aforesaid"—American Archives, 5th series, vol. 1, pp. 1507-1508.

This case is one of special interest. It shows that the New York Colony

did not hesitate to imprison "a young woman" detected in "a dangerous act." And the imprisonment was directed to be in jail; and to continue until she complied with the requirements of the Congress.*

---

* A council of military officers, viz: William Heath, Joseph Spencer, Nathan Green, and Sterling, with the approval of General Washington, complained of the discharge of tories upon their bonds, and recommended some more effectual method of securing good behaviour.—*Ibid*, 1435.

## CHAPTER III.

### WRIT OF HABEAS CORPUS.

From the documents relative to the Colonial History of the State of New York found in Holland, England and France and collected by John R. Brodhead, vol. iii, it appears that the *act* of Habeas Corpus was not extended to that colony. If then the Writ of Habeas Corpus existed prior to the contest with the crown, it was as a common law right.

However this may be, there is no evidence that the Provincial Congress made any provision for its operation; nor does it seem to have been a subject of special legislation until the 21st Feb., 1787.

Nor is this all. The *organization and practice* of the Provincial Congress and Committees, would not allow of the existence of the Writ. For as was said, in an adopted report to the former body, made on the 31st of May, 1776—

"Of necessity in many instances Legislative, Judicial, and Executive powers have been vested in *them*, especially since the dissolution of the form of government by the abdication of the late Governor, and the exclusion of this Colony from the protection of the King of Great Britain."

It is true that in *some* cases appeals from the determinations of the Committees, Special or General, to the Provincial Congress or Committee of Safety were authorized, but these were not controlled by "the doctrines of the writ of *habeas corpus*." In proof

the following from numerous instances may be cited:

"In Committee of Safety, &c., December 6th, 1776, Capt. Platt, from the Committee to whom the case of Mr. Abraham C. Cuyler, late Mayor of the city of Albany, was referred, applied to this Committee to know whether they should *examine into the original cause* of his commitment, or only inquire whether he had broken his parole; and if it should appear that he had, order him to be sent to Connecticut, or such other place of confinement as the Committee may think proper.

"*Resolved*, That if it shall appear that Mr. Cuyler has broken his parole in leaving Connecticut, that he be ordered by the Committee to such place of confinement as they may think proper, and that if he has reason to complain of hard treatment in his original commitment, this Committee will at their leisure inquire into it, and do him ample justice; but they will not authorize any persons, under pretence of obtaining a rehearing, to break their paroles or condemn the power by which they were committed.

"*Resolved unanimously*, That the Representatives of this State in Committee of Safety assembled, do agree with the said Committee for detecting and defeating conspiracies in their said report."—*American Archives*, 5 series, vol. 3, p. 360.

This is both pertinent and conclusive; it shows that an inquiry into the *original cause* of commitment was unauthorized, and that such inquiry was not regarded as a matter of right, but as an act of discretion to be exercised, if at all, not without delay but at leisure.

It is thus clear that the writ of *ha-*

*beas corpus* was inoperative, both *eo nomine* and in spirit or pratice in New York during the existence of its temporary or original forms of government.

# CHAPTER IV.

1. On the 21st of May, 1776, it was proposed by a committee, acting in relation to "intestine enemies," that it would be

"Proper to take the assistance of his Excellency General Washington, and to march several detachments of the troops under his command into Queen's county, and DISARM the inhabitants, excepting those who shall subscribe the following declaration, viz:

"We, the subscribers, inhabitants of —— in Queen's county, in the Colony of New York, do voluntarily and solemnly engage, under all the ties held sacred amongst mankind, at the risk of our lives and fortunes, to defend by arms the United American Colonies against the hostile attempts of the fleets and armies belonging to or in the pay of Great Britain, until the present unhappy controversy between the two countries shall be terminated, etc."

It was also proposed "that all such persons as are required as aforesaid to be DISARMED, shall, on *pain of imprisonment*, take the following oath, or, being of the people called quakers, the following affirmation:

I, A. B., do swear (or solemnly affirm and declare) that I have *not now in my possession, nor in the possession of any other person or persons, or deposited or secreted* in any place or places, any *arms* which have not been delivered up to this Committee or their order; neither have I the arms of any other person or persons, or for any use or purpose whatsoever, now in my possession, so help me God.—*American Archives*, 4th series, vol. 6th, *p.*

These propositions appear to have been approved. The *second* exacted "an oath of discovery" from the persons who refused to subscribe the declaration. And in accordance with it individuals were imprisoned, as appears from the proceedings of the Congress of the 3d of June, 1776:

"A letter from Augustus Van Horne, Vincent P. Ashfield, John L. C. Roome, and Thomas W. Moore, all confined in jail by order of the General Committee of New York, *for refusing to sign* the declaration, or *deliver up their arms on oath* as directed by the resolution of the late Provincial Congress, was read and filed."—*Ibid*, 1359.*

* In June, 1776, General Washington was requested to take the most speedy and effectual method to disarm, etc., disaffected persons of Nassau Island.

# CHAPTER V.

## INTERFERENCE WITH CORRESPONDENCE OR SEIZURE OF PRIVATE PAPERS.

These acts were not unusual. One instance will be given; it will be found in the following quotation from a letter of the Convention to Governor Trumbull, of Conn., dated Wednesday morning, August 28th, 1776:

"We now take the liberty of enclosing to your Honor, the copy of an *intercepted letter* from D. Matthews, Esq., to his wife, from which it appears that he deeply resents the reatment he received from the Convention. t is with the utmost regret that we feel ourselves under the necessity of requesting your Honor to secure that gentleman in such manner as to prevent his escape, and all improper correspondence. The troubling you with our prisoners is a matter for which necessity alone can apologize. This State has suffered so much from disaffected persons, that a greater degree of severity towards them would be justifiable, especially as all lenity hath been by them attributed to fear. Notwithstanding such high provocation, we have in no instance invaded the rights of humanity, it might, therefore, be expected that we should be surprised to see such a designed misrepresentation of our conduct, but nothing of this kind is new. The crime of which Mr. Matthews stands charged is no less than treason against the rights of America, and yet it seems he considers his confinement as unjust."—*American Archives, 5th series, vol. 1, p.* 1551.

It seems that not even a letter to his wife, "the sacred correspondence of the holy relation created by marriage," was allowed "to pass unnoticed and unexamined."

## CHAPTER VI.

### DOMICILIARY VISITS, OR SEARCHING OF PRIVATE HOUSES.

The searching of private houses for various purposes was frequent. The extent to which it was allowed will be seen from this extract :

THURSDAY AFTERNOON,
*July* 11, 1776.

" Convention met pursuant to adjournment.
" On motion resolved, that the general committee of the county of Tryon be, and they hereby are, authorized and requested to employ proper persons to take the leaden

weights out of all the windows in said county, and apply so much thereof as may be immediately necessary to the use of the militia of said county."—American Archives, 5th series, vol. I, p 1397.

Compliance with this resolution involved not only entrance into houses, but a close search. And this is only one of a series of resolutions which authorized an examination of individual dwellings, and the removal from them of property.

## CHAPTER VII.

### RESTRAINT UPON TRAVEL OR INTERFERENCE WITH THE JOURNEYING OF PRIVATE PERSONS.

The annexed proceedings will furnish a clear conception of the manner in which the New York convention controlled the journeying of individuals.

The following resolutions moved by Robert R. Livingston, Esq., were read and agreed to, viz :

" As great abuses are daily committed in the granting of *passes* without sufficient examination to persons inimical to the State, in order to remedy the same as well as to prevent and detect counterfeit passes,

" *Ordered*, That every county committee throughout this State appoint two judicious men of known attachment to its interest in each precinct, manor, or district, who shall grant the passes hereinafter mentioned to such persons only of whose principles they shall be fully satisfied :

" *Ordered*, That four thousand passes be printed, leaving a blank for the date, name, and place of abode of the person, and the place to which he may proceed ; that they be signed by either of the secretaries of the convention of this State, and sent to the several counties, to be lodged in the hands of the commissioners above mentioned :

" *Ordered*, That when any person shall

apply for a pass the blank in the same shall be filled up with his name in the handwriting of the person so applying, and the commissioner granting shall endorse the same :

" *Resolved*, That from and after the twentieth day of this month no person be permitted to travel out of the district, manor, or precinct in which he usually resides, unless he comes from some other State, and brings a pass for the same, without such a pass as above described, or such as may be granted by the Convention, or Committee of Safety of this State ; but shall be liable to be arrested and detained by any member of either county, district, manor, or Precinct Committee, or any military officer, till discharged by order either of the Committee of the district, manor, or precinct in which he was so arrested, or by the general committee of the county in which he is detained."—American Arch., 5th series, vol. 3, pp. 300, 301.

The restraint thus imposed on travel was, in all respects, complete. And to render it effectual, arrests and imprisonments by individuals, committees, and military officers were permitted.

# CHAPTER VIII.

## The Control and use of Private Property.

The power claimed in relation to private property was without limitation.

It included these particulars: Temporary impressment, removal, destruction, and permanent use.

### 1. Temporary use.

"*Resolved*, That the Secret Committee have power to impress boats, vessels, teams, wagons, horses, and drivers, when they shall find it necessary for the public service, as well as to call out the militia, if occasion should require."—Amer. Arch., 5th series, vol. I, p. 1411.

### 2. Removal.

"The committee appointed to confer with General Washington relative to the stock on Long and Staten Islands reported in the words following, to wit:

"That all the cattle, horses and sheep, on Staten Island, (except such as those hereafter mentioned,) be removed with all expedition. But as some milch cows and horses are indispensably necessary for the subsistence of the inhabitants, it was agreed that two hundred horses be left for the use of the inhabitants, no one person keeping more than two. The milch cows be kept in the following proportions, and not to be exceeded, viz: Three for a large family, two for a middling family, and one for a small family. No person to be permitted now to keep a cow who has not done so for two months past."—Amer. Arch., 4th series, vol. VI, p. 1439.

### 3. Destruction.

"And, *ordered*, that General Woodhull and the said committee (Mr. Hobart and Mr. James Townsend) be and hereby are instructed that they cause all such *stock* and all such *grain* in Queen's county, and the western part of Suffolk county, as may be in danger of falling into the enemies hands, and cannot be removed to places of safety, to be destroyed."—Ib., vol. 1, 1549.

### 4. Permanent use.

"*Resolved*, Unanimously, that the committee of Safety and Correspondence at New York be appointed and authorized to take from the doors of the houses in the city of New York all the brass knockers, and that they cause the same to be sent to some careful person at New Ark, in New Jersey, with all possible despatch."—American Archives, 5th series, volume II, p. 669.

# CHAPTER IX.

## Confiscation of the Property, Real and Personal, of Tories.

1. On December 3, 1776, "the Committee of Safety"

"Ordered that Mr. Duane, Mr. Moore, and Mr. R. R. Livingston, be a committee to devise an ordinance for securing all estates and effects which are *deserted* by the owners, or which though under the care of others belonging to the enemy, or who have absconded."—Amer. Arch., 5th series, vol. III, p. 347.

2. On the 9th of the same month,

"An inventory of the *real and personal* estates of sundry persons in the town of Salem who have gone over to the enemy, dated December 6th, 1776, and signed by Exekiel Hawley, Chairman of the Committee of said town, was read and filed."

In reply, "the conduct of the committee of Salem was highly approved," and they were informed—

"That the committee have under consideration a report for the security and disposal of all estates under the like circumstances. It will not be long before you shall be furnished with these regulations." American Archives, 5th series, volume III, p. 364.

Finally on the 22d of October, 1779, an act was passed entitled

"An Act for the forfeiture and sale of the estates of persons who have *adhered to the enemies* of this State, and for declaring the sovereignty of the people of this State, in respect to all property within the same."

A part of the *preamble* was in these words:

" And whereas the *public justice* and *safety of this State* absolutely require that the most notorious offenders should be immediately hereby convicted and attainted of the offence aforesaid, in order to work a forfeiture of their respective estates and vest the same in the people of this State."

The first section provided that John Murray, Earl of Dunmore, formally Governor of the Colony of New York, William Tryon, late Governor of the said Colony, (and others who were named,)

" Be, and each of them are hereby severally declared to be, *ipso facto*, convicted and attainted of the offence aforesaid ; and that all and singular the estate, both real and personal, held or claimed by them the said persons severally and respectively, whether in possession, reversion, or remainder, within this State on the day of the passing of this act shall be and are hereby is declared to be forfeited to and vested in the people of this State."—*Laws of New York, Greenleaf's Edition, vol.* 1, *pages* 26, 27.

In these cases no summons, no notice, no trial was allowed. The conviction and forfeiture were summary and unconditional. The subsequent sections of the act provided a plan for the convictions and attainders of " other offenders" than those mentioned in the first section.—*Ibid, pages* 27, 38.

And on the 12th of May, 1784, an act was passed entitled

"An Act for the speedy sale of confiscated and forfeited estates within the State, etc."

This was the preamble :

Whereas, the public exigencies require that the goods and chattels, lands and tenements which have been forfeited to, and are now vested in the people of this State by attainder or conviction, in the progress of the late war, should be sold and converted into money, and otherwise applied for sinking and discharging the public securities.—*Ib.*, p. 127.

The XXIII section reads thus:

" That all forfeitures and confiscations of the lands, tenements, hereditaments, and real estate which heretofore have been by virtue of any former law or laws of this State against any person or persons whomsoever, on conviction for adhering to the late enemies of this State, or of this and the other United States of America, is and are hereby to all intents, constructions, and purposes in the law whatsoever, fully and absolutely ratified and confirmed, notwithstanding any error or errors in the proceedings thereon, or in any wise relating thereto, and all writs of error and errors on any judgment hereto rendered relating thereto, are hereby forever barred."—*Ib.*, p. 139.

Neither imbecility nor bigotry can demand more satisfactory proof of the facts that New York promptly adopted the principle of confiscation, and that she sanctioned and continued it after the close of the revolution.

## CHAPTER X.

### CONTROL OF ELECTIONS.

That none who were hostile to " the Colonies" were allowed to vote, appears from different portions of the proceedings of the " Congress or Convention" and of the " Committees," but this section of the Constitution of 20th of April, 1777, only will be quoted:

" VIII. That every elector before he is admitted to vote, shall if required by the returning officer or either of the inspectors, to take an oath, or if of the people called quakers, an affirmation of *allegiance* to the State.—*Laws of New York, Greenleaf's Edition, vol.* 1, *p.* 8.

# CHAPTER XI.

## REFUSING CONTINENTAL MONEY.

The subjoined extract from the proceedings of the Provincial Congress of the 28th of May, 1776, is full and complete on this topic :

"Capt. Thomas Harriot being called before this Committee, was duly convicted of *having refused to receive* in payment the Continental bills, and still persist in refusing the same. * * * * * *
This Committee conceiving the said Thomas Harriot to be a dangerous person do request that the Provincial Congress may acquaint them if they think he ought to be suffered to go at large, as he is now in the custody of the guard.—New York Committee Chamber, May 28th, 1776.
"By order of the Committee :
  ROBERT HARPER, Deputy Chairman.
" To the Honorable the Congress of the Colony of New York."

"*Resolved*, That the General Committee of the city of New York be requested and authorized, and are hereby requested and authorized, to direct that Thomas Harriot *be immediately committed to close jail in this city, there to remain until further order of this Congress.*"—American Archives, 4th series, vol. 6th, p. 1344.

The determination to sustain "the Continental money" was certainly inflexible ; and an effort to prevent this being done was regarded as an offence which should be justly punished.

# CHAPTER XII.

## RELIGION AND POLITICS.

In a letter addressed to the Hon. John Hancock, Esq., President of the Continental Congress dated White Plains, Westchester county, July 11, 1776, this paragraph occurs :

"We take the liberty of suggesting to your consideration also the propriety of taking some measures for expunging from the Book of Common Prayer such parts, and discontinuing in the congregations of all other denominations all such prayers as interfere with the interest of the American cause"—American Archives, 5th series, vol I, p. 1396.

This is conclusive. Prayers in public which tended to operate against the Colonies in their contest for independence, it was suggested, should not be permitted.

Nor was there any hesitancy to "lay hands upon divines" who did not saction that contest?  And therefore this preamble and resolution :

"Whereas the Rev. Samuel Seabury, of the borough of Westchester, is notoriously *disaffected* to the American cause, and from his vicinity to the enemy has opportunities of rendering them essential service :
" *Resolved*, That Col. Joseph Drake be directed *forthwith to remove* the said Samuel Seabury from Westchester to the house of Col. John Brinckerhoff at this place, to remain there till the further order of the Convention, or Committee of Safety, of this State ; and that he be not permitted to leave the farm of the said Col. John Brinckerhoff except in company with the Col."—American Archives, 5th series, volume II, p. 683.

# CHAPTER XIII.

## RIGHT OF SPEECH AND LIBERTY OF THE PRESS.

The extent to which interference with "the right of speech and the liberty of the press"* was deemed proper will be shown by these extracts :

The proceedings of the Committee of Observation were misrepresented in Rivington's Gazétte on the 2d of March, 1775, and a committee consisting of *Philip Livingston* and *John Jay* were appointed to wait on the proprietor and editor, James Rivington, to ascertain by whose authority or on whose information his mistatements were made.

The response was "from common report," and it was then

"*Resolved*, That common report is not sufficient authority for any printer in this city to publish any matters as facts relative to this Committee. * * * *
"Ordered, That the foregoing order, report, and resolve be forthwith printed in all the papers.
"By order of the Committee:
"Isaac Low, Chairman."
[American Archives, 4th series, vol. 2, pages 50, 51.]

The action of the Committee, however, had little or no influence on Mr. Rivington, and he continued to assail and traduce the colonies. He was therefore censured in every section of the country.

In New Windsor, Ulster county, March 14th, 1775, this action was had:

"And further, we consider the freedom of the press as the great palladium of English liberty; therefore, we'll do all in our power to encourage and support *the same*. But there is a certain news-printer in New York, named James Rivington, who appears to us divested of every principle of honor, *truth*, or modesty; his paper being filled with pieces *replete with falsehood and mere chicanary*, only designed, as we believe, to divide and lead estray the friends of our happy Constitution:
"*Resolved*, therefore, 6th nem. con., That we will have no connection or intercourse with said Rivington, nor will we purchase any of his publications until we receive sufficient evidence of his sincere repentance."
* * American Archives, 4th series, vol. 2, p. 132.

At length, however, Mr. Rivington "recanted," confessed his error, and the Provincial Congress then adopted this preamble and resolution, viz:

"Whereas James Rivington, of this city, printer, hath signed the General Association, and has lately published a handbill declaring his intention rigidly to adhere to the said association; and also asked the pardon of the public who have been offended by his ill-judged publications:
"*Resolved*, therefore, that the said James Rivington be permitted to return to his house and family; and that this Congress doth recommend it to the inhabitants of this Colony not to molest him in his person or property."—Amer. Arch., vol. 2, 4th series, p. 1284.

Thomas Willet, Sheriff of Queen's county, was imprisoned for *certifying and publishing* a "declaration of Richard Viscount Howe, and William Howe, attested by William Tryon, late Governor.—Amer. Arch., vol. I, p. 1467.†

*The use of the phrases "*right of speech*," and "*liberty of the press*," in this connection is not deemed strictly correct; yet the common usage is followed. Properly considered, these were not "interfered with." It was *licentiousness* of speech and of the press, an *abuse* of their liberty which was condemned.

The distinction indicated should be more generally presented or maintained. It is a neglect of this that often imparts plausibility to the declamation prevalent on these subjects. A *right* should always be supported and vindicated; an *abuse* of a right should always be discouraged and condemned.

†William Waine for "propagating divers false reports calculated to injure the American cause," was committed to jail.—Am. Arch., 5th series, vol. I, p. 683.

## CHAPTER XIV.

### CONTROL OF STATE MILITIA.

It is familiar to all that the most persistent efforts have been put forth by the present Executive of the State of New York to prevent the National Government from making a draft within her territory, or from obtaining control of her militia.

In these efforts he has been sustained by the factionists who have been associated with him; and the position has been assumed and discussed that the military force of the States should be kept under the immediate command or management of the local authorities.*

But no such contracted opinion prevailed in the New York Convention of 1776.

On the 11th of July of that year it addressed a letter "to John Hancock, Esq., President of the Continental Congress" in which this paragraph occurred:

"Sir: In pursuance of a resolution of your honorable House of the 17th of June last, we have passed a resolve to authorize the Commander-in-Chief to call out all or any part of our militia whenever he might think it necessary, of which we enclose you a copy.—" * * * (Am. Arch., 5th series, vol. 1, p. 1395 )

The 'request' of the Continental Congress, it thus seems, met with a favorable response, and the New York militia were promptly placed under the orders of the Commander-in-Chief. And it is fair to presume that this concurrent action—the rule which it sanctioned, agreeing as it did with that of other Colonies—was subsequently adopted by the framers of the National Constitution; and thus an inferential argument is furnished in favor of the construction, given its provisions relative to the " militia " of the several States, by the supporters of the administration.

Their position is simply this: that the General Government in periods of war, internal or foreign, has primary and ultimate control of those " who are liable to be called out into her service." And it has been practice in harmony with this position, which has evoked much of the im. passoned declamation which has been uttered in relation to "conscriptions, drafts, and State right."

But why continue these extracts? In Convention of the Representatives of the State of New York, at White Plains, July 9, 1776, it was

"Resolved, That the Delegates of this State in Continental Congress be, and they are hereby authorized to consent to and adopt all such measures as they may deem condusive to the happiness and welfare of the United States of America."

And throughout the revolutionary era, her various assemblies acted in accordance with this principle, adopting without hesitancy such approved measures as tended to promote and secure " the welfare of the people."

And in view of this fact; in view of the citations collated from her early records, what apology can be offered for the intimation—the substantial assertion—of Horatio Seymour, in the Academy of Music, on the 4th of July, 1863, that "our own forefathers" would not have suspended, what he denominated personal rights and personal liberties.*

Was it stolid ignorance or base design that prompted the assertion? Others may determine.

*This is the ultimate opinion of George W. Woodward, of Pennsylvania, and the class of judicial politicians whom he represents.

* As appears from the context of his speech, he included in these expressions: "freedom from arbitrary arrests," sacredness of houses, liberty of speech, etc., etc. The very things which New York, " our own fathers," did " suspend" and absolutely control.

## PENNSYLVANIA.

The formal or associated movements of Pennsylvania for "the security of the rights of the colonies," commenced in 1775.

The powers of Government were exercised primarily by a " General Assembly" and "a Supreme Executive Council."

As early as June 30, 1775, a Committee of Safety, finally styled a Council of Safety, was appointed.

The minutes of these several assemblies will be the source from which extracts will be taken.

# CHAPTER I.

## ARBITRARY ARRESTS.

The annexed extracts from the proceedings of the General Assembly of Pennsylvania, passed 13th of October, 1777, entitled

"An act for constituting a Council of Safety, and vesting the same with the powers therein mentioned,"

Will be satisfactory in relation to arrests.*

Be it * * * enacted, &c., * * * That the members of the Supreme Executive Council of this State, together with John Bayard, Jonathan Seargent, Jonathan B. Smith, David Rittenhouse, Joseph Gardner, Robt. Orndt, Curtis Grubb, James Cannon, William Henry, of Lyncaster, Esq., be constituted, and they are hereby constituted *a Council of Safety*, with full power to promote and provide for the preservation of the Commonwealth by such regulations and ordinances *as to them shall seem neccesary*, and to procede against, *seize*, detain, imprison, punish either capitally or otherwise as the case may require, *in a summary mode*, either by themselves, or

others by them to be appointed for that purpose, all persons who shall disobey or transgress the same or the laws of this State heretofore made for the purpose of restraining or punishing traitors or others who, from their general conduct and conversation, may be deemed inimical to the common cause of liberty and the United States of North America.

*And be it further enacted*, &c., That the members of the said Executive Council and the said John Bayard et al., or any other persons acting under their authority in the premises, or any of them, shall not at any time hereafter be liable to any suit, action, or prosecution for any thing done in pursuance of this act, or the powers hereby given and granted, but that they shall be indemnified, saved harmless, and discharged of the same, &c.

By the authority of this act arrests could be made *ad libitum*, and "in a summary mode," and not only of "known traitors," but also of those whose general conduct or conversation created a suspicion of disloyalty. And anticipating that "as in these latter days," arrested individuals would allege that it was wrongly done and institute suits to recover *damages*, the Geneaal Assembly provided that none should be recovered; thus throwing a shield of protection against "the true and the loyal."

---

* The arrests made both before and after the date of the act were numerous, and included "all classes of the inhabitants of the colonies" They were made with and without warrants for "overt acts," and on *mere suspicion;* and when no armed enemy was in the colony, as well as when it was invaded by the British forces.

# CHAPTER II.

## IMPRISONMENT.

The number of State prisoners in Pennsylvania was large.

The Continental Congress on the 31st July, 1777, recommended to "the Supreme Executive Council—

Forthwith to make prisoners, such of the late Crown and proprietary officers, and other persons in and near this city, as are disaffected or may be dangerous to the public liberty, and send them back into the

country, there to be confined or enlarged upon parole as their characters and behavour may require.

That it be recommended to the said Executive Council to remove under guard, all the State prisoners in the goal of this city, to some safe place in the country, and that they cause the guards to be doubled until the prisoners can be removed.—Penn. Archives, vol. 5, p. 469.

On the succeeding day, a warrant was issued directed to the Board of

War,* based on the request of Congress for the arrest of the persons it had designated and others.

In this warrant or order this comprehension clause occurred :

"And you are hereby further empowered to *imprison*, remove, confine, and enlarge on their *parole* as you see fit, all persons whatsoever whom you may *know or suspect to be disaffected to and inimically disposed against the United States of North America*, or against this Commonwealth, &c."—Ib., p. 478.

More extended powers could not possibly have been conferred, and many were immediately arrested and imprisoned. The places of imprisonment were various. A considerable number were removed to Virginia. Some were committed to jails, some to Free masons lodge in Philadelphia, others and among them several women, were confined in the State prison.—Ib., p. 336, 37.

* The Board of War consisted of nine persons, viz: David Rittenhouse, Owen Biddle, William Moore, Joseph Dean, Samuel Morris, sr., Samuel Cadwallader, W. Cerris, John Bayard, George Gray, and John Ball, Esqs., appointed on the 13th of March, 1777.

They had "full power and authority to do and perform all matters and things necessary" in the land service of the State, subject to the direction of the Supreme Executive Council.—Minutes of the Supreme Executive Council, vol. 11, p. 181.

## CHAPTER III.

### Writ of Habeas Corpus.

In 1777 a writ of *habeas corpus* was issued for the release of a number of persons who had been arrested by order of the Supreme Executive Council, and directed to be sent to Winchester, Virginia. The officer in charge of the prisoners disregarded the writ, and reported the fact to the Council of Safety, and the General Assembly immediately passed a bill indemnifying the Executive Council and those acting under its authority, and suspending the writ of *habeas corpus*.

This was done on the 16th of September, 1777. The title of the bill was

"An Act to empower the Supreme Executive Council of this Commonwealth to provide for the security thereof, in special cases, where no provision is already made by law."

The relevant part of it was in these words:

"*And be it further enacted*, That the President, Vice President, and other members of the Supreme Executive Council of this Commonwealth, and all persons acting by their special command in the premises, shall be and are hereafter fully indemnified and saved harmless from all process, suits, and actions that shall or may be hereafter sued, commenced, prosecuted, or brought against them, or any or either of them, for or in respect of any of their orders or proceedings heretofore issued and had upon the recommendation of Congress, or which they shall hereafter issue and have by virtue of this act. And that no judge or officer of the Supreme Court, or any inferior court within this Commonwealth shall issue or allow of any writ of *habeas corpus*, or other remedial writ, to obstruct the proceedings of the said Executive Council against suspected persons in this time of imminent danger to the State; provided always, and it is hereby further enacted by the authority aforesaid, that this act shall be in force to the end of the first setting of the next General Assembly of this Commonwealth and no longer."—(Law Book, No. 1, pp. 137-138.

This act accords with the English practice, and shows what the views of Pennsylvania were at the time of the Revolution concerning the writ of *habeas corpus*.

Her "wise men" and patriots could not, would not, allow the proceedings of the *Executive* council against *suspected* persons at a period of *imminent danger* to the country to be obstructed by any intervention or process of the courts. The dogmatism and denunciation of modern declaimers, it might be supposed, would be softened, if not terminated, by this fact; but, unfortunately, intellectual perversion superinduced by morbidness and dishonesty of heart, cannot be corrected by any degree of information.

# CHAPTER IV.

## SEIZURE OF ARMS.

This was most explicitly directed. Hence the Supreme Executive Council—

" *Resolved,* That the colonel or commanding officer of each regiment of the city militia do appoint one or more officers, and a sufficient number of men in each ward, who shall *search the houses* of all such of the "inhabitants of the city of Philadelphia who have not manifested their attachment to the American cause, *for firearms, swords, and*

*bayonets.*"— * * * * Min. Sup. Ex. Coun., vol. XI, p. 279.

Similar quotations could be given, but this sufficiently evinces that the Executive Council considered that the right to bear and possess arms was *conditional not absolute ;* or, in other words, that the presence or absence of attachment to the cause, which *it* represented, determined the right.

# CHAPTER V.

## INTERFERENCE WITH CORRESPONDENCE, OR SEIZURE OF PRIVATE PAPERS.

The extent to which this interference or seizure was authorized will fully appear from a section of the act of 16th of September, 1777. It will be given in full.

" Be it therefore enacted, and it is hereby enacted by the representatives of the freemen of the Commonwealth of Pennsylvania, in General Assembly met, and by the authority of the same, that it may and shall be lawful for the President or Vice President, and the members of the Supreme Executive Council of this State, or any two of them, either upon the recommendation of Congress or at the requisition of the Commander-in-chief of the army, or the commander of a division or corps in the same, or upon the information of any credible subject of this or any other of the United States, to arrest any person or persons within this Commonwealth who shall be suspected, from any of his or her acts, writings, speeches, conversations, travels, or other behavior, to be disaffected to the community of this, or all, or any, of the United States of America, or to be an harbinger of the common enemy who is at our gates, or to give mediate or immediate intelligence and warning to their commanders by letters, messengers or tokens, or by discouraging people from taking up arms for the defence of the country, or spreading false news, or

doing any other thing to subvert the good order and regulations which are or may be pursued for the safety of the country, AND TO SEIZE AND EXAMINE SUCH PAPERS IN THEIR POSSESSION AS SHALL IN ANY WISE AFFECT THE PUBLIC ; and, the same persons being arrested, to confine and remove them to any distant place, where it will be out of their power to disturb the peace and safety of the States ; or to tender to them the oath or affirmation of allegiance or fidelity to the State, as directed by law, and, upon taking or subscribing the same, to enlarge them, or to demand and take such other and further security and assurance from them as the said President or Vice President and Council, or any two of them, in their discretion shall think proper, or as the particular circumstances of the case may require."

This entire section should be carefully considered. There is scarcely a point of importance which it does not cover.

Its words of *immediate pertenancy* however are given in capitals. Few they are, but demonstrative ; and acting in accordance with them "the proper persons" seized and examined both letters and papers. So they should still do.

# CHAPTER VI.

## DOMICILIARY VISITS, OR SEARCHING OF PRIVATE HOUSES.

For various purposes the searching of private houses was authorized. An ordinance was passed in October, 1777, by " the Council of Safety" appointing commissioners to make inventories of all the personal effects of those inimical to the cause of the Colonies, etc. It concluded thus:

"And be it lastly resolved, ordained and declared by the authority aforesaid, that the said commissioners, or any or either of them, shall be fully authorized and empowered to *search* for and seize the said goods and effects of such offenders, and for this end to send for, call before them, and examine, persons and papers, to use force, and to break open doors in all cases where the same goods may be secreted and concealed, to commit such as shall absolutely resist their authority, and to call to their aid officers and others, civil and military, who are hereby required and commanded to aid and assist them accordingly.—Min. Sup. Exec. Coun., Rec., vol. XI, pp. 330, 331.

This resolution "went as far" as the most earnest and daring could desire; permitting not only a "*search*," but a breaking of doors, the use of force, and also an arrest of all who might resist, or oppose, these acts.

## CHAPTER VII.

### RESTRAINT UPON TRAVEL.

The "danger to be apprehended from persons traveling without any test of loyalty," was carefully guarded against.

The "Supreme Executive Council therefore

"*Resolved*, That no person be suffered to go over the west side of Schuylkill, unless they produce a pass signed by Benjamin Paschall, Esq., or William Hayshaw, or unless they produce a certificate of their having taken and subscribed an oath or affirmation of allegiance to this or the United States of America; but persons bringing provisions to market are to be permitted to pass and re-pass without interruption."—Min. Sup. Ex. Coun., vol. XI, p. 298.

Other and corresponding resolutions were adopted, but they need not be produced.

## CHAPTER VIII.

### IMPRESSMENT AND USE OF PRIVATE PROPERTY.

These, among other orders, emanated from the Council of Safety. On the 27th of August, 1777,

"That the justices of the county of Philadelphia be *required* to send down immediately twenty-five wagons, and that the justices of the county of Chester be required to send down twenty-five wagons, to be subject to the orders of the Quartermaster General or his agents."—Min. of the Sup. Ex. Coun., vol. XI, p. 279.

And on the 31st of August:

"That Gen. Armstrong employ proper persons to purchase blankets of all persons disposed to sell, for the use of the militia.

"That if such purchases seem impracticable, to make as equal and moderate a levy of blankets as circumstances will permit, upon the inhabitants of the county of Chester, in this State, for the use of the militia, confining the same to persons who refuse to bear arms, or take an active part in the defence of their bleeding country." * * Ib., pp. 284, 285.

These "ordinances" referred to teams and blankets, but almost every description of property was subordinated to the use or management of the State, or its associated colonies.

## CHAPTER IX.

### CONFISCATION OF THE PROPERTY, REAL AND PERSONAL, OF TORIES.

On the 5th of September, 1776, an act was passed entitled, "An ordinance of the State of Pennsylvania declaring what shall be treason, and for punishing the same, and other crimes and practices against the State."

After a preamble in these words:

"Whereas Government ought at all times to take the most effective measures for the safety and security of the States," it ordained and declared "that all and every * * * * person and persons * * owing allegiance to the State of Pennsylvania, who from and after the publication hereof, shall levy war against the State, or be adherent to the King of Great Britain or others, the enemies of this State, or to the enemies of the United States of America, by giving him or them aid or assistance within the limits of this State or elsewhere, and shall be thereof duly convicted in any court of oyer and terminer hereafter to be erected according to law, shall be adjudged guilty of high treason, and forfeit his lands, tenements, goods, and chattels, to the use of the State, and be imprisoned any term not exceeding the duration of the present war with Great Britain, at the discretion of the judge or judges."— Amer. Ar., 5th ser., vol. II, p. 35.

Acts more minute in their provisions were passed on the 11th of Febuary, 1777, on the 21st of October, 1777, and at other periods.—(Laws of Pennsylvania, vol. 1, p. 436,) Min. Sup. Ex. Com., vol, 11, p. 329.

In accordance with the practice under these acts, proclamations were issued requiring the persons named in them to appear before "one of the Justices of the Supreme Court, or of one of the counties of the State, and abide a trial for adhering to or assisting her enemies, on pain of being attainted of treason and of the forfeiture of their real and personal estate. In one of these proclamations upwards of four hundred persons were named, in another over two hundred ; and their estates confiscated.

# CHAPTER X.

## INTERFERENCE WITH ELECTIONS.

The qualifications of voters became a subject of deliberation at an early period of the contest with George the III. They were determined by a Provincial Conference of Committees, which assembled at Carpenter's Hall in Philadelphia in June, 1776.

1. No one was allowed to vote except an *associator* of the age of twenty-one years. But if required to do so by a judge or inspector, it was necessary for him to take the following test on oath or affirmation, viz :

"I, ——, do declare that I do not hold myself bound to bear allegiance to George the III, King of Great Britain, &c., and that I will not, by any means, directly or indirectly, oppose the establishment of a free government in this province by the Convention now to be chosen, nor the measures adopted by the Congress, against the tyranny attempted to be established in these colonies by the Court of Great Britain."— Am. Arch., 4th se., vol. 6, p. 953.

2. Persons of *known or proclaimed* hostility to the liberties of America were entirely disfranchised by this regulation :

*Resolved unanimously*, That no person who has been published by any Committee of Inspection or the Committee of Safety in this province as an enemy of the liberties of America, and has not been restored to the favor of this country, shall be permitted to vote at the election of members for said Convention.—Ib., 4th se., vol. 6, p. 54.

3. Besides, attempts on the part of tories to hold or control elections did not pass unnoticed.—Min. Sup. Prov. Coun., vol. 5, pp. 31, 32, 53.

That these adopted regulations would encounter considerable opposition was anticipated. The anticipation became a fact. Riots occasionally occurred.— Ibid, 53.

Nor did the objections urged against the *prescribed oath* differ from those which are now advanced against similar tests of loyalty. Referring to *it*, John Hubly in a letter to President Wharton, dated Lancaster, July, 1777

"I am much mistaken in my judgment if this very oath of abjuration and allegiance * * * will not be the very foundation on which new objections will arise * * * and you will hear a loud cry against this tyrannical oath, that it was intended for naught but to hinder substantial, good disposed people to elect or be elected, depriving them of the rights of freemen," &c.—Penn. Arc., vol. V, p. 427.

Subsequent utterances or developments showed that he was not "mistaken." It is at least true, then, of evil—of the utterances of treason—that there is "nothing new under the sun." And if poetic genius be correct, the essential reasoning of the American rebels of 1864, and their northern confederates, dropped from the lips of Satan in his contest with Jehovah. It is "old and base stuff."

## CHAPTER XI.

### SPECULATION IN CONTINENTAL MONEY, OR DEPRECATING OF PUBLIC CREDIT.

This was not for a moment tolerated. Therefore it was

*Resolved*, That all persons (to whom debts are now or shall henceforth become due) who shall refuse to accept continental money from his or their debtors in discharge of such debts), it being first properly tendered to them in the presence of two witnesses, shall, and they are hereby forever barred from the recovery of such debts, and are hereby ordered to deliver up any bond, bill, or note upon which such debt may become due unto the said debtor or debtors, and the pains and penalties of fine and imprisonment, &c.—Penn. Archives, p. 126.

The stringency of this resolution could not well be surpassed. Certain it is it would not have been adopted, had it not been deemed of *great importance*, to sustain the general currency.

## CHAPTER XII.

### RELIGION AND POLITICS.

In 1777, Rev. Mr. Coombe, an assistant minister of "Christ's and St. Paul Church, Philadelphia," was arrested and imprisoned.

On the 9th of September, the corporation of the Rector's Church Warden and Vestryman presented the following representation to the Supreme Executive Council:

GENTLEMEN: Being truly alarmed and concerned at hearing that Rev. Mr. Coombe, one of our assistant ministers, had been arrested in his own house, and removed from thence, and put under confinement, we, appointed a committee to wait upon him in order to satisfy ourselves by what authority he was made prisoner, what charge had been brought against him, whether he had applied for a hearing, and whether a hearing had been granted. His answer by the Committee was: "That he was confined by a resolve of the President and Council of Pennsylvania, formed in consequence of a recommendatory resolve of Congress. That the general charge was his having evinced a disposition inimical to the cause of America; that he had joined with some respectable fellow-citizens, who were imprisoned with him, in an application for a hearing; that a hearing had not been granted, but that he was informed by a messenger from the Council, that he is to be sent to Augusta county in Virginia."

We beg leave to observe to you, gentlemen, that the connexion betwixt ministers and people hath, in every Christain State, been deemed a tender and spiritual one; an attempt to dissolve this connexion by the removal of a minister upon a general charge without suffering him to know his accusers, or being heard in his own defence cannot but be deemed an infringment of religious as well as civil liberty.

The respect we have for Mr. Coombe, and the duty we owe to our constituents, the members of the two Episcopal Churches in this city, whom we have the honor to represent, will not permit us to be silent on this occasion. We do, therefore, as well for ourselves as in the name and behalf of these respectable congregations, earnestly request it of you as you regard the civil and religious rights of freemen, and the present Constitution of Pennsylvania from whence alone you derive your authority as a council, that Mr. Coombe be admitted, as his undoubted birthright, to an hearing in the face of his country.

Not suffering ourselves to doubt of your cheerful compliance with this most reasonable request, we are gentlemen, with all due respect, your humble servants,

JACOB DUCHI, Rector,

THOS. CUTHBERT, } Wardens.
JAMES REYNOLDS, }

Signed by order of Vestry, Philadelphia, September 9, 1777.

This representation is given in full:

1. It accused the Supreme Executive Council with an infringement of religious and civil liberty and of the Constitution of Pennsylvania.

2. It rested the accusation upon two facts and an assumption. The facts were these: first, that the arrest of Mr. Coombe had been made upon a *general complaint*, and second, that he had been refused a hearing. The assumption was this: that the sacredness of the ministerial relation was such as to preclude any interference with it by the civil power unless, perhaps, in extraordinary cases, or under peculiar circumstances.

Now what was the response of the Council? It was in these words:

GENTS: It is with concern that the Council have read an address from the Rector, Church Wardens, and Vestry of the united Episcopal Churches of Christ's Church and St. Peter's Churches in the city of Philadelphia, concerning the Rev. Mr. Coombe. *His case is wholly political.* They would be sorry your corporation should draw imputations on them by this application.

I am directed to inform you, that Council had, before this piece came, *determined* to send away Mr. Coombe and the rest of the prisoners, and that his connection with your congregation can be no argument in his behalf.

Instead of admitting that there was any cogency in either of the positions of the "representation"—far from conceding that ministers of the gospel possessed a sanctity, a refined spirituality which elevated them above ordinary mortals, and placed them beyond the range of governmental power—it asserted that MR. COOMBE'S *case was wholly political*, that there was no necessary antagonism between his *profession* and treason, that his conduct

sustained this truth, and that, therefore, he was not entitled to a hearing, nor to a release from the custody of the State.

But while the Supreme Executive Council did not hesitate to make this response, to declare that a divine might be a traitor, and be justly subject to the penalties of his crime, it was not because there was any want of respect or veneration for "the man of God" in Pennsylvania.

Far otherwise was it, as the "circular" addressed by "the Committee of Safety" to the "clergy" determines:

"REV'D SIR:

"Your country greatly depends on the encouragement which you give to your people. We doubt neither your virtue, patriotism, nor readiness, to contribute all in your power to animate them in the cause, and induce them to march to the assistance of General Washington. If you or any of your brethren would offer to go as chaplain to the militia it would have an exceeding good effect. The Council of Safety, solicitors for the event of the present campaign, entreat you to exert all your well known influence and abilities in the service of your country.—Penn. Arch., volume V, p. 83.

And what was the response of the *majority* of the clergy to this circular? It was one of approval, of co-operation with the civil powers in their important contest for human rights and liberties.

So that it may be safely affirmed that neither the one nor the other considered that "in serving the country the minister of the Gospel degraded his office, or stepped out of his appropriate sphere."

This is an idea which derives whatever strength or speciousness it has from the impulses and sophistries of disloyalty, and not from the pages of the Bible.

## CHAPTER XIII.

### TEST OATHS.

1. These were exacted from all officers, civil and military.—Min. | Sup. Ex. Coun., vol. XI, pp. 174, 292, 417.

2. They were required from individuals engaged in private pursuits, and from suspected persons.

The following was taken by one of eht latter class :

" In Council of Safety,
30th Aug., 1776.

"I do swear on the Holy Evangelists of Almighty God that I will not take up arms against the United States of America, nor hold any correspondence with, or give any intelligence to, the enemies of the said States ; and that I will not contrive any plots or treasonable practices against the said States ; but will inform the Council of Safety of Pennsylvania of all such practices as may come to my knowledge, as witness my hand this 30th Aug., 1776.—Penn. Ar., vol. V, p. 15.      FRANCIS MILLS."

Let it be noted that this was an obligation first to refrain from acts hostile to the "United States of America ;" and, second, to assist them by furnishing information of the existence of such acts.

And why should not a similar obligation be imposed upon " the indifferent, the neutrals, the suspected," in the present crisis ? It could not do any injury or wrong, it might be productive of good ; unless, indeed, those to whom it should be administered have "lost all consciousness with regard to the binding force of an oath."

## CHAPTER XIV.

### Right of Speech and Liberty of the Press.

Story, in commenting on the clause of the Constitution (Amendment, art. I,) which prohibits Congress from making any law abridging freedom of speech, or of the press, says :

" That this amendment was intended to secure to every citizen an absolute right to speak, or write, or print whatever he might please, without any responsibility, public or private therefor, is a supposition too wild to be indulged by any rational man."

And, he proceeds to add, that upon this supposition

" A man might stir up sedition, rebellion, and treason, even against the Government itself, in the wantonness of his passions, or the corruption of his heart. Civil society could not go on under such circumstances."

And subsequently he affirms :

"That the exercise of a right is essentially different from an abuse of it. The one is no legitimate inference from the other. Common sense promulgates the broad doctrine, sic utere tuo, ut non alienum lodas ; so exercise your own freedom as not to infringe the rights of others, or the public peace and safety."—Story on the Constitution, § 1880, 1888.

These, obscured, suppressed, peverted as they have recently been, are un-

questionably the only correct views of " freedom of speech or of the press," which an enlightened or virtuous community or government should entertain or sanction. And it admits of no intelligent doubt, that they are the views which prevailed in the Colony of Pennsylvania. Here is some of the proof :

I. "An ordinance respecting adversedly writing and speaking against the American cause, was read the first time and ordered to lay on the table for a second reading. —(Pro. Penn. Prov. Com., Sept. 6th, 1776) Am. Arch., 5 series, vol. 2., p. 35.

2. In harmony with this ordinance was the 4th section of

" An Act declaring what shall be treason, and what other practices and crimes against the State shall be misprison of treason," passed 11th of February, 1777.

The act was preceded by this important preamble :

" Whereas it as absolutely necessary for the safety of every State to prevent as much as possible, all treasonable and dangerous practices that may be carried on by the internal enemies thereof, and to provide punishment in some degree adequate thereto, in order to deter all persons from the perpetration of such horrid and dangerous crimes."

It then rendered acts which it enumerated punishable as treason and others as misprison of treason. Among the latter were this :

*" Publicly and deliberately speaking or writing against our public defence."*

The penalty, for thus speaking or writing was

"Imprisonment during the present war and a forfeit to the Commonwealth of one-half of the tenements, goods and chattels of the offender."—Laws of Penn., vol. 1, p. 436.

3. It is true under this act *a formal conviction* was required ; but it did not do away with summary arrests and imprisonment. Moreover, the form of conviction does not affect the nature of crime, nor alter the opinion of the law maker in relation to it.

It is chiefly the penalty which gives a conception of the light in which he regarded the offense.

If this be so, it is manifest that the colonists of Pennsylvania, her " men of renown and of civil lore," considered " speaking and writing *against* the public defence" or their measures and principles, as highly culpable. To an extended, " *licentious*" degree they would not tolerate it.

Here the extracts from " the Archives of Pennsylvania" must close.

The candid and unbiased mind will not fail to derive from them correct conceptions of the mode in which that State sustained and carried on the contest for freedom against " internal enemies."

## MARYLAND.

Maryland was prompt and energetic in her advocacy and support of " the rights of the Colonies, and of the principles of the Declaration of Independence."

Her principal assembly was " a Convention," composed of " deputies from the several counties." Subordinate to the Convention was a Council of Safety, and County Committees of Observation."

Her records are less voluminous than those of New York and Pennsylvania ; but, as will be immediately seen, they are of no less pertinency and importance.

## CHAPTER I.

### ARBITRARY ARRESTS.

Arrests were not unfrequent in Maryland. They were sometimes made directly by the Convention, or in compliance with its order; but generally by the Committees of Observation, or the Council of Safety.

Special authority was given to the latter body to secure, and in fact dispose of, those disaffected and hostile to the American cause, as will appear from the following resolution passed by the Convention on the 15th of January, 1776.

"*Resolved,* * * * That the said Council of Safety have power and authority to *arrest*, and, on hearing, confine and imprison till the next Convention, all such persons within this province as shall have been, or may be, guilty of high and dangerous offences, tending to disunite the people of this province in their present opposition, or to destroy the liberties of America ; and also have power and authority to bear, try and imprison till the end of the next Convention, or banish all such offenders, guilty of the offence aforesaid, as may be sent to them by the several Committees of Observation."—Am. Arch., 4th se., vol. 4, p. 760.

It will be at once observed that the power thus conferred, was absolute and unrestricted, and it was exercised without any particular reference to forms or precedents. Maryland was not encumbered by these in arresting those " guilty of high and dangerous offences against the liberties of America." And in her judgment *neutrality* was an offense, as well as the outbursts of unrestrained opposition to the purposes of the Colony, or sympathy with the designs and schemes of the mother country.

# CHAPTER II.

## IMPRISONMENT.

1. The power given the Council of Safety in the resolution quoted in the preceding chapter authorized it not only to arrest but "to *confine and imprison*."

By a prior resolution passed in August, 1775, *a part* of the Council "residing nearest to the place where an offence was committed, was authorized to examine charges, and if satisfied of their truth to pronounce sentence thereon," and that the

"Person be *imprisoned* in such place and manner; and for such time, as shall be adjudged, not beyond the rising of the next Convention, who, if they think proper, may take further order therein; or that he depart this province within a certain time to be limited."—Amer. Archives, 4th ser., vol. III, p. 115.

2. On July 26, 1775, a form of association was adopted "to be signed by the members of the Convention, and all other freemen," of the Province of Maryland.

It contained this important clause:

"And we do unite and associate as one band, and firmly and solemnly engage and pledge ourselves to each other, and to *America*, that we will to the utmost of our power promote and support the present opposition carrying on, as well as by arms as by the Continental Association restraining,

our commerce."—Amer. Arch., 4th series, vol. III, p. 108.

On the 16th of July, 1776, it was ordained that

"Any person refusing to sign the said Association, etc.,    *    *    *    and continuing to reside within the Province may be *imprisoned* by the Committee of Observation of the county in which such non associator resides, or may be found, until the Convention then next after such *imprisonment* shall have taken order thereon."—Ib., vol. IV, p. 756.

In the judicious use of the powers thus given, both the Council of Safety and the Committee of Observation imprisoned various persons.—Ib., vol. III, pp. 1569, 1589, vol. VI, p. 1457.

3. But the Convention possessing original power as the representatives of the loyal people of the entire Province, ordered the imprisonment of a considerable number of the suspected or dangerous inhabitants.—Ib., vol. IV, pp. 714, 719, 722.

Among the offences for which the Convention imprisoned was "suspicion of attempting to convey intelligence to Lord Dunne, and reflecting upon the proceedings of the Convention."

The instances of imprisonment could be largely increased, but it is not deemed important to do so.

# CHAPTER III.

## WRIT OF HABEAS CORPUS.

From the commencement to the termination of the revolutionary struggle the writ of Habeas corpus does not appear to have been in use in Maryland. The fact is, its desuetude was *ex necessitate rei* required, and there was therefore a tacit acquiescence in its *practical* suspension until 1777.

In February, however, of that year, as a precautionary measure, to prevent the purposes of the Colony from being delayed or obstructed by the courts, the Habeas corpus act in case of the invasion of the State was for-

mally suspended by the XII section of

"An act to punish certain crimes and misdemeanor, and to prevent the growth of Toryism," passed in February, 1777.

The words of suspension were these:

"And that during any invasion of this State by the enemy the habeas corpus act shall be suspended, as to all such persons (those dangerous to the safety of the State) arrested by order of the governor or council."—Kilty's Laws of Maryland. vol. I.

# CHAPTER IV.

## SEIZURE OF ARMS.

To the greatest extent the seizure of arms was authorized.

On the 27th of March, 1776, Mr. Tilghman transmitted to the "Council of Safety" a resolve of Congress, relative to the DISARMING of non associates and persons disaffected to the cause of America.

Thereupon it was ordered, that copies thereof be sent to the several Committees of Observation in each county and district in this Province, respectively.—Am. Arch, 4th series, vol. 5, p. 1552.

On June 28th, 1776, the Convention on reading a letter from the Committee of Observation for Sommerset county,

*Ordered*, that Major Price take command of, and direct so many of the Independent Companies on the Eastern shore, to march immediately to the lower part of Sommerset county, as he may think proper; and that if necessary, he be assisted with, and command such of the militia as shall be called on by a Committee to be appointed by this Convention; that he proceed to *disarm* all such persons in that county as shall, from good grounds, appear to such Committee to be disaffected, and to take into custody all such disaffected persons, etc.—Ib., vol. 11, pp. 1490, 1491.

John Platter and John Hill were appointed the Committee referred to in the above order, and they were invested with power to *disarm* similar to that conferred on Major Price.

Others were clothed with the same power.—Ib., 4th vol., 1723, 5th vol., 1513, 1515, 1529, 6th vol., 1458.

Hence the erroneous idea, that those who are positively opposed to a great national struggle, or indifferent to it, should be allowed to retain and collect arms, derives no sanction from the "old and pure records" of Maryland. And it should not be omitted here, that Capt. William Cromwell in May, 1776,

"Took from Harry Dorsey Gough, Esq., a non associate and non enroller, seven and a half pounds of powder," with the approbation of the Baltimore County Committee.—Ib., vol. 6th, p. 1459.

Baltimore *then* declared that neither arms nor ammunition should be in the hands of "the enemies of the country."

# CHAPTER V.

## INTERFERENCE WITH CORRESPONDENCE OR SEIZURE OF PAPERS.

The Continental Congress on the 16th of April, 1776, requested the Council of Safety to seize the person and papers of Alexander Ross, and that the papers be sent safely to the Congress. Proceeding immediately to comply with the request, on the 20th of April it was

Ordered, that Alexander Ross be brought before the Council at three o'clock in the afternoon.

He was examined and remanded back into custody.

And thereupon, ordered, that the said Alexander Ross deliver to Col. Smallwood's order, all and singular *his papers*, of what

sort soever, now at Daniel Grant's Tavern in Baltimore town.

*Ordered*, that the officers appointed to bring Alexander Ross's papers from Baltimore town have full power to *take possession of the said Ross's portmanteau*, and all the papers lodged with Mr. Grant, and to convey the same to the Council.—Am. Arch., 4th series, vol. 5, p. 1563.

And on the 25th of April, his papers were sent to Congress "as also his person under guard."—Ib., p. 106.

In the same year, letters to Robert Eden, Governor of Maryland, were intercepted and examined; and the Convention approved of the action of the Council of Safety in reference to the correspondence.—Ib., p. 928.

# CHAPTER VI.

## DOMICILIARY VISITS, OR SEARCHING OF PRIVATE DWELLINGS.

It will not be asserted that there was any inclination in Maryland, to invade the sacredness of private life, yet there was no reluctance, no delay in searching dwellings when it was suspected or believed they were used to promote in any manner the designs of the enemies of the United Colonies. In corroboration of this statement a single instance, taken from the proceedings of the Baltimore County Committee, of July 14, 1775, will be furnished:

" A *report* having been circulated that a number of arms, and a quanity of ammunition were secretly lodged in the house of Mr. James Christie, and the same being mentioned to the Committee, they directed two of their members, Capt. Clopper and Mr. James Cox, *to go immediately and search Mr. Christie's house;* which they accordingly did, and reported that they had examined the house attentively in every part, attended by Mr. Robert Christie, jr., and that they only found two guns and a pair of pistols, and no ammunition, and were convinced no others were in the house."—Amer. Arch., 4th series, vol. 4, p. 1723.

Attention should be fixed upon the fact that this search was based upon a *mere report.* This report was supported by " oath or affirmation." No warrant was issued. Capt. Clopper and James Cox were simply directed to make the search, and in accordance with this direction, it was attentively made.

That it failed to sustain the report, was a consideration of no consequence. It was still regarded as justifiable—" a measure of precaution, looking to the welfare of the people."

# CHAPTER VII.

## RESTRAINT UPON TRAVEL OR INTERFERENCE WITH THE JOURNEYING OF SUSPECTED PERSONS.

This restraint was exerted in two respects:

1. In prohibiting individuals from leaving the Province. For this purpose, the Convention on the 24th of June, 1776, on motion

*Resolved,* that no *passport* to leave America be granted by the Council of Safety to any person not an inhabitant of this Province, unless such person *produce a passport* from the Assembly, Convention, Committee, or Council of Safety of the Colony where such person did last reside.

2. In regulating or preventing travel *within* the Province. The surveillance in this particular was close, and continued. Hence on the 7th of November, 1776, the Convention on the application of Mrs. Chamier for leave to visit her husband, in General Howe's camp,

*Resolved,* that Mr. President be requested to write to the honorable, the President of the Congress, to grant a passport for Mrs. Chamier to go to the American camp, with a recommendation to his Excellency General Washington to grant his permission for Mrs. Chamier to visit her husband, on giving her parole of honor not to say or do anything to the injury of the United States or any of them."—Amer. Arch., 5th series, vol. 3, p. 162.

Woman's footsteps, as well as man's, were placed under " guard and guide."

# CHAPTER VIII.

## IMPRESSMENT OR USE OF PRIVATE PROPERTY.

Various articles of personal property, belonging to individuals, appear to have been seized and used for the benefit of the Colonies in Maryland, such as guns, shoes, and boats.

H ere, however, is an instance in which property of another class was taken, at least, temporarily:

" It appearing to this House that Robert Browne, the proprietor of the warehouse on the land of the late Charles Browne, * * hath refused to let the said warehouse for the purpose of carrying into execution a resolve of this House of the 6th of September lust,

*Resolved*, that the Inspector immediately take possession of the said warehouse for the purpose aforesaid, and the Committee of Observation of said county are hereby required, if it shall be necessary, to be aiding and assisting in enforcing this resolution, and for that purpose to call in the force of the county, or any part thereof."—Amer. Arch., 5th series, vol. 3, p. 115.

## CHAPTER IX.

### CONFISCATION OF THE PROPERTY, REAL AND PERSONAL, OF TORIES.

On a day which will be forever memorable in the history of America, the 4th of July, 1776, the Convention

*Resolved*, that if *any inhabitant* of this Colony shall after the 5th of August next, within or without this Colony * * * levy war against the United Colonies or any of them, etc., etc., such persons on conviction thereof * * * * * shall suffer death without benefit of clergy, and *forfeit all the estate which he had at the time of the commission of the crime* to be applied to the use of the Colony, etc.—Am. Arch., 4th se., vol. 6, p. 1500.

This was only, however, initiative, for as Sabine correctly asserts in his work entitled "The Loyalist of the American Revolution," vol. 1, p. 80:

"Maryland seized, confiscated, and appropriated all property of persons in allegiance to the British Crown, and appointed Commissioners to carry out the terms of three statutes which were passed to effect these purposes."—Kilty's Laws of Md., Oct. 1777, 1780-82-84.

## CHAPTER X.

### INTERFERENCE WITH ELECTIONS.

Few are so rash, or so unwise, as to maintain that there should be no interference by a free government with the elective franchise. But a wide difference of opinion appears to exist as to what should be the extent and manner of the interference.

It may therefore be well to produce with some minuteness the views of Maryland on this point during the sublime and heroic contest of the Colonies.

1. She suppressed an attempt to hold elections under the Proprietary or English government. This was done by her Convention of Deputies June 25th, 1776.

The minute in relation to it reads thus:

"The Convention being informed that writs of election have been issued in the name of the Proprietary for the election of delegates in Assembly,

"*Resolved*, That the said writs be not obeyed, and that no election be made in consequence thereof."—Amer. Arch., 4th series, vol. VI, p. 1487.

2. She determined that "no enemy

to the liberties of America should be allowed to vote in the election of representatives to form a new government by the authority of the people only."

The prohibition was in these words:

"That no person who has been *published* by any Committee of Observation, or the Council of Safety of this Colony, as an enemy to the liberties of America, and has not been restored to the favor of his country, shall be permitted to vote at the election of members for the said Convention."—Ib. p. 1497.

It was adopted by the Convention July 3, 1776, and enforced.

3. She required all persons friendly to America to assist the judges of elections in Kent and Worcester counties.

This was done by resolutions of the Convention of August the 15th, 1776. That in relation to Kent county was as follows, viz:

"*Resolved*, That all friends to America, and the interest, peace, and happiness of this Province, are required, if necessary, to be aiding and assisting to the judges of election for Kent county in the execution of their office, and this Convention will support and maintain the said judges in the discharge of their duty."—Amer. Arch., 5th series, vol. III, pp. 85, 86.

That, relative to Worcester county was exactly similar, except that it contained an explicit pledge of support to those who might render the judges necessary assistance.

In order, however, that these resolutions be fully comprehended, two historic facts connected with them must be mentioned.

1. The remote occasion of their passage was "base and impertinent conduct" at the period of the regular election for Representatives to the Convention to form a new government.

This conduct proceeded from persons opposed to the measures of the Colonies, and prevented an election in the first named county, and rendered it void in the other.

2. The immediate consideration which led to their adoption was an anticipated repetition of this conduct.

To these facts must be added two important observations of more than common applicability to the present times.

1st. The clause or words all friends to America, etc., *ex vi termini* included soldiers. It is therefore undeniable that they were not only permitted, but required, to assist the judges of the election, if necessary, in the performance of their duties.

2d. This assistance was directed or ordered for the purposes of preventing the disaffected and inimical from interrupting the elections, or controlling them by their votes.

What a perfect justification is thus furnished, of the action of "the military powers," relative to the election of Maryland and of the Test Oath prescribed by the late Constitutional Convention!

## CHAPTER XI.
### RELIGION AND POLITICS.

It has been affirmed that in none of the Colonies did there exist a more profound regard for the religious element or sentiment than in Maryland; yet she would not allow Ministers of the Gospel to array themselves against her opposition to the policy of Great Britain. Among those who were arrested for so doing, was Rev. John Scott and Rev. John Bowie, D. D. Nor were clergymen simply arrested; they were censured, fined, or incarcerated.

Maryland was not, however, content with thus disposing of "disaffected and dangerous divines." She did far more. On the 25th of May, 1776, the Convention

" *Resolved*, that every prayer and petition for the King's Majesty, in the *book* of common prayer and administration of the sacraments, and other rites and ceremonies of the church, according to the use of the church of England, except the second collect for the King in the communion service be henceforth *omitted* in all churches and chapels in this Province until our unhappy differences are ended."—Am. Arch., 4th se., vol. 5, p. 1598.

This is clear. It shows that she claimed and exercised the *right* to suppress religious rites and ceremonies and public prayers—when they did not coincide with the designs and measures of the Colonies.

That this should still be done, is a proposition which within the three last years has elicited considerable discussion and even coarse invective.

It is difficult, however, to conceive any sound reason which can be advanced against it. Certain it is, that it is sustained by the 33d Article of the present Declaration of rights of Maryland. It, allows unmolested worship of God,

"Unless, under color of religion, any man shall disturb the good order, peace, or safety of the State, or shall infringe the laws of morality, or injure others in their natural, civil, or religious rights."

Religion, true piety, asks no shield, no protection for either of these wrongful acts. It is hypocracy, " a form of godliness without the power," which puts forth this demand.

## CHAPTER XII.
### RIGHT OF SPEECH OR LIBERTY OF THE PRESS.

Maryland in repeated instances, and in the most unequivocal mode declared that "the right of speech" should be restrained and regulated.

Two of the instances in which she did this may be referred to:

1. Rev. John Patterson reflected upon the proceedings of the Convention, asserted "that it was depriving men of their liberty; that the last Convention had treated James Christie in a tyrannical, cruel and oppressive manner; and that there was more liberty in Turkey than in this Province," etc.

The Convention upon ascertaining these facts.

"*Resolved*, that the Committee of Observation for Kent county take into custody the Rev. John Patterson, and send him to this Convention."—American Archives, 4th series, vol. IV, p. 714.

He was finally censured by the President "for the indecency and intemperance of his expressions," and discharged upon an acknowledgment of his offense, and on payment of the expense of the proceedings against him."—Sabine's Loyalists, vol. 2, p. 152.

2. Francis Sanderson was "guilty of delivering sentiments tending to discourage the American opposition to the hostile attempts of Great Britain,"

And it was decided by the Convention

"That, therefore, he be reprimanded at the bar of this House by the President; that he give bond in the penalty of one thousand pounds, with good security, to be approved of by the Committee of Baltimore county, to the President, conditioned that he will not hereafter *speak*, or do any matter or thing, in prejudice or discouragement of the present opposition," &c.—Amer. Ar., 5th series, vol. III, p. 125.

These instances are too plain and pertinent to be distorted or assailed.

The expressions of Rev. Mr. Patterson, and the sentiments of Mr. Sanderson, it will be observed, differ not in spirit or character, but in object, or the personality of their reference from the utterances of modern clerical and lay traducers and denunciators of the Government, and of the measures employed by it to suppress the Rebellion.

History, it has been said, reproduces itself. It seems that biography does the same.

More cannot be conveniently added from *the proceedings* of the Maryland Convention,\* or its Council of Safety, or Committees of Observation

Enough, however, has been gathered from them, to show that she did not "handle her domestic enemies — her fireside foes — with gloved hands, or attempt to cure their disease either by large or infinitesimal doses of conciliation and gentleness."

———

What, then, appears? Exactly what it was proposed to establish.

FIRST, THAT THE OPINIONS AND ACTIONS OF THE CONTINENTAL CONGRESS AND OF THE COLONIES OF NEW YORK, PENNSYLVANIA, AND MARYLAND IN THE GREAT STRUGGLE, PRIMARILY FOR "THEIR RIGHTS AS BRITISH SUBJECTS" AND ULTIMATELY FOR NATIONAL INDEPENDENCE, WERE NOT ANTAGONISTIC BUT HARMONIOUS; AND, SECOND, THAT AS THE PRESENT ADMINISTRATION IS JUSTIFIED IN ITS PRINCIPLES AND MEASURES BY THE FORMER, SO IT IS BY THE LATTER; IN FACT, BY BOTH THEIR UNITED AND SEPARATE UTTERANCES AND DEEDS.

THIS, IS STRONG SUPPORT. THIS, IS AMPLE VINDICATION.

———

\* That the archives of other States contain "matter no less relevant and demonstrative" than those of New York, Pennsylvanio, and Maryland, will be evident from this extract from "an Act" of Virginia, passed in May, 1781:

"Whereas, in this time of public danger, it is necessary to invest the executive with the most ample powers.  *  *  *

The governor, with advice of the council is also hereby empowered to apprehend, or cause to be apprehended and committed to close confinement, any person or persons whatsoever, whom they may have just cause to suspect of disaffection to the independence of the United States, or of attachment to their enemies, and such person or persons shall not be set at liberty by bail, mainprize, or *habeas corpus*."—Heuning's Statutes at Large, vol. 10, p. 414.

# PART III.

The ultimate or collective opinions of deliberate assemblies, ordinarily, are surperior to those of individuals. This in fact, is only a modification or distinctive form of the aphorism " that in the multitude of Counsellors there is safety."

Yet, in intellectual investigations, the separate opinions of distinguished thinkers, scholars, moralists, or patriots should not be disregarded or overlooked. They are often valuable and entitled to great defference and consideration.

In accordance, therefore, with the plan enunciated, extracts from the writings of some of the heroes and sages of "the days that tried mens souls" will be produced.

These, however, will be brief, and confined to a few of the most important topics. Moreover, analogous and to some extent, distinct topics will be placed in the same chapter. This will be done in order to present one or two points of no small interest and value, which otherwise it would be necessary to omit.

## CHAPTER I.

### ARBITRARY ARRESTS AND IMPRISONMENT.

" As it is now very apparent that we have nothing to depend on in the present contest, but our own strength, care, firmness, and union ; should not the same measures be adopted in your and every other Government on the continent ? Would it not be prudent to *seize* on those tories who have been, are, and that we know will be, active against us ? *Why should persons, who are preying upon the vitals of their country, be suffered to stalk at large, whilst we know they will do us every mischief in their power ?* These, sir, are points I beg to submit to your serious consideration."—George Washington to Gov. Trumbull ; Writings of Washington, vol. 3, p. 159.

" It was *indecision* that has thrown your affairs in Virginia into their present situation; had my opinion been thought worthy of attention, Lord Dunmore should have been disarmed of his teeth and his claws. I proposed seizing Tryon and all his tories at New York. * * * You will justly accuse me of self-conceit and egotism, but I have not yet done.

I propose, therefore, the following measures: " First. To seize every Governor, Government man, placeman, tory, and enemy to liberty on the continent ; to confiscate their estates, or, at least, lay them under heavy contributions for the public; their persons should be secured in some of the interior towns as hostages for their treatment of those of our party whom the fortune of war shall throw into their hands, etc."—Gen. Lee to Richard Henry Lee ; Am. Arch., 4th se., vol. 4, pp. 248, 249.

## CHAPTER II.

### SEIZURE OF ARMS.

" The tories should be *disarmed* immediately, though it is probable that they may have secured their arms on board the King's ships until called upon to use them against us. However, you can seize upon the persons of the principals. They must be so notoriously known, that there will be little danger of your committing mistakes, and happy should I be if the Governor could be one of them."—Gen. Washington to Major Gen. Lee ; Washington's Writings, vol. 3, p. 273.

" The spirit of disaffection which appears in this country, I think, deserves your serious attention. Instead of giving any assistance in repelling the enemy the militia, have not only refused to obey your general summons and that of their commanding officers, but I am told exult at the approach of the enemy, and on our late misfortunes. I beg leave, therefore, to submit to your consideration *whether such people are to be trusted with arms in their hands.*"

And he adds :

" In my opinion we ought not to hesitate a moment in taking their arms."—General Washington to the Council of Safety of Pennsylvania, Bucks county, 15th Dec., 1776 ; Spark's Washington, vol. 4, pp. 223, 224.

# CHAPTER III.

## LIBERTY OF THE PRESS AND RIGHT OF SPEECH.

In his letter to Gov. Cooke of Connecticut, Washington enumerates an act of that Colony declaring that "none should *speak, write*, or act against the proceedings of Congress, or their acts of Assembly, under penalty of being disarmed and disqualified for holding any office, and being further punished by imprisonment," as one which met his approbation, and which should exist in other colonies."—Writings of Washington, vol. III, p. 228.

In the commencement of the Revolution it was discovered by the Orange county, Va., committee that "a Rev'd Mr. Wingate was in possession of various pamphlets reflecting very injuriously on the conduct and motives of the Continental Congress, and in other respects adverse to the public cause." The committee peremptorily demanded the pamphlets, obtained and examined them, and passed the following resolution, which William C. Rieves says was "the production, doubtless, of their accomplished penman, (James Madison,) and instinct with the spirit he had early imbibed in defence of American rights."

"*Resolved,* That as a collection of the most audacious insults on that august body (the grand Continental Congress) and their proceedings, and also on the several colonies from which they were deputed, particularly New England and Virginia, of the most slavish doctrines of provincial government, and of the most impudent falsehoods and malicious artifices, to excite divisions among the friends of America, these pamphlets deserve to be publicly burnt as a testimony of the committee's detestation and abhorrence of the writers and their principles."—Rieves's Life and Times of Madison, vol. I, p. 96.

Action in accordance with this resolution, it appears, immediately followed; for Mr. Rieves says:

The record then continues, "which sentence was speedily executed in the presence of the Independent Company of Orange, and other respectable inhabitants of said county, all of whom joined in expressing a noble indignation against such execrable publications, and their ardent wishes for an opportunity of inflicting on the authors, publishers, and abettors, the punishment due to their insufferable arrogance and atrocious crimes."

# CHAPTER IV.

## BANISHMENT OF TORIES AND CONFISCATION OF THEIR ESTATES, ETC.

"I am informed that the Connecticut Assembly are very unanimous in the common cause; and, among other acts have passed one for raising and equipping a fourth of their militia * * * Another act for restraining and punishing persons inimical to us, and directing proceedings therein, etc., etc. * * * Another act for *seizing and confiscating* for the use of the Colony the estates of those putting or continuing to shelter themselves under the protection of the ministerial fleet or army, or *assisting them in carrying on their measures against us.*" * * * The situation of our affairs seems to call for regulations like these, and I should think the other Colonies ought to adopt similar ones, or such of them as they had not already made."—Washington to Gov. Cooke, January 6th, 1776; Spark's Washington, vol. 3, p. 228.

"There can be little doubt that every society may rightfully banish from among them those who aim at its subversion, and forfeit the property which they can only be entitled to by the laws, and under the protection of the society which they attempt to destroy."—Letter of Robert R. Livingston to Benjamin Franklin, 7th January, 1782; Franklin's Works, vol. 9, p. 139.

"But we differ a little in our sentiments respecting the loyalists, (as they call themselves,) and the conduct of America towards them. * * * Even the example you propose of the English Commonwealth's restoring the estates of the royalists after their being subdued, seems rather to countenance and encourage our acting differently, as probably if the power which always accompanies property had not been restored to the royalists, *if their estates had remained confiscated,* and their persons had been banished, they could not have so much contributed to the restoration of kingly power, and the new Government of the Republic might have been more durable."—Franklin in a letter to Francis Maseres, dated Pasay, June 26, 1785.—Works of Franklin, vol. 10, pp.191, 192.

# CHAPTER V.

## COERCION OR USE OF FORCE BY THE GENERAL GOVERNMENT.

"Vigorous ones, (*i. e.* measures,) and such as at another time would seem extraordinary are now become absolutely necessary," etc.—Washington in 1776; Spark's Washington, vol. 3, p 329.

"The necessity of arming Congress with coercive powers arises from the shameful deficiency of some of the States, which are most capable of yielding their apportioned supplies, and the military exactions to which others, already exhausted by the enemy, and our own troops are in consequence exposed. Without such powers, too, in the General Government, the whole confederacy may be insulted, and the most salutary measures frustrated by the most inconsiderable State in the Union."—Madison to Jefferson, 16 Ap., 1781. Life by Rieves, p. 304.

"As the Confederation now stands," and according to the nature even of alliances much less intimate, there is an implied right of coercion against the delinquent party, whenever a palpable necessity occurs.—Ib. History of the Republic of the United States by Hamilton, vol. 2, p. 230.

"The words of the Constitution are explicit, that the Constitution and laws of the United States *shall be* supreme over the constitution and laws of the several States; supreme in their exposition and *execution*, as well as in their authority. Without a supremacy in those respects, it would be like a scabbard in the hands of a soldier without a sword in it."—Madison to W. C. Rieves, March 12, 1833.

It has been so often said, as to be generally believed, that Congress have no power by the confederation to enforce anything; for example, contributions of money. It was not necessary to give them that power expressly; they have it by the law of nature. When two parties make a compact there results to each a power of compelling the other to execute it.* Compulsion was never so easy as in our case, where a single frigate would soon levy on the commerce of any State the deficiency of its contributions."—Jefferson to Col. Edward Carrington; Memoirs of Jefferson, p. 203.

"That there may happen cases in which the National Government may be under the necessity of resorting to *force*, cannot be denied. Our own experience has corroborated the lessons taught by the examples of other nations; that emergencies of this sort will sometimes exist in all societies, however constituted; that seditions and insurrections are, unhappily, maladies as inseparable from the body-politic, as tumors and eruptions from the natural body; that the idea of governing at all times by the simple force of law, (which we have been told is the only admissible principle of republican government) has no place but in the reverie of those political doctors, whose sagacity disdains the admonitions of experimental instruction. Should such emergencies at any time happen under the National Government, there could be no remedy but force. The means to be employed must be proportioned to the extent of the mischief."—Hamilton in No. 28 of The Federalist.

"Fellow-citizens : civil war is, undoubtedly a great evil. It is one that every good man would wish to avoid, and will deplore if inevitable. *But it is incomparably a less evil than the destruction of Government.* The first brings with it serious but temporary and partial ills : the last undermines the foundations of our security and happiness, *and where should we be if it once were to grow into a maxim, that force is not to be used against the seditious combinations of parts of the community to resist the laws ?* This would be to give a Carte Blanche to ambition, to licentiousness, to foreign intrigue, to make you the prey of the gold of other Nations —the sport of the passions and vices of individuals among yourselves.

The Hydra Anarchy would rear its head in every quarter. The goodly fabric you have established would be rent asunder and precipitated into the dust."—Hamilton's Works, vol. VII, p. 166.

Such then are some of the opinions of Washington, Lee, Livingston, Franklin, Madison, Jefferson, and Hamilton. To amplify them, to extend them to other topics, to add to them the views of Henry, Randolph, Sherman, Adams, Morris, Jay, Wilson, Pinckney, and others, "who though dead yet speak," would not be difficult; but it would be unnecessary—a useless piling of Ossa on Pelian and Olympus on Ossa. *For with sufficient clearness*

---

*The intelligent reader will not fail to observe the *force* of this extract and the first from Madison. It is conceded that the confederacy was "abandoned because of the weakness of its powers, and that the substituted government was given greater strength." If so, and the Confederacy possessed compulsory power, a *fortiori*, the present Government possesses it.

and copiousness of quotations, it is shown that the individual opinions of the fathers of the Republic coincided with the organized or combined views of the Continental Congress, and the Colonial or State Conventions, Councils or Committees.

And in addition to this, it is fully established that Mr. Lincoln or his Administration, has most profoundly studied and persistently regarded the sentiments of these great apostles of liberty and expounders of the rights of man.

In the footsteps which they placed in the sands of time, as a guide for "their children and childrens' children," has he cautiously walked.

By the beacon lights which they kindled to save the ark of our freedom from hidden dangers and engulphing waves, has he been warned and directed. And hence, while faction impugns his motives and misrepresents his purposes; while ambition and interest stigmatize his opinions; while ignorance coarsely sneers at his deeds and stupidly misunderstands his words; while treason detests his principles and denounces his firmness, it remains an unassailable, inflexible, immutable truth, that from the venerated Council Chambers of the architects of our Nationality—from the pens of the wise and heroic of the first age of the Republic—from all of the noble, the pure, and the good of the past, there come voices of approval and words of encomium.

Thus sustained, thus eulogized, to every vituperative assault upon his policy and malignant traduction of his untarnished character, he may respond—

" 'Tis but the fate of place, and the rough brake
That virtue must go through."

A true and patriotic people—the grand march of human events—the controling hand of God in the history of the world and of "the days of agitation and conflict which are upon us," will not fail to justify the response, and to complete the vindication.

☞ Let it be remembered, that in the preparation of this tract, there has been no attempt to present to the reader any of the graces or beauties of rhetoric. It is its plan, its facts, its arguments, and its suggestions which claim attention.

www.ingramcontent.com/pod-product-compliance
Lightning Source LLC
Chambersburg PA
CBHW030900260626
47169CB00008B/2618